Project Renovatio

by Allison Maruska

allisonmaruska.com

This book is a work of fiction. Names, characters, places and incidents are products of the author's imagination or are used fictitiously. Any resemblance to actual events or locales or persons, living or dead, is entirely coincidental.

Cover Art: Carolina Fiandri – Circecorp
(www.circecorpdesign.com)

Advance Praise for Project Renovatio

What if scientists take genetic engineering to the next level and start altering the human race? Allison Maruska writes a thrilling YA novel that will grab the attention of her readers and hold it until the end. In Project Renovatio, Levin Davis and his two sisters live a seemingly normal life. They have a mom and step-dad, they are very well educated, and Levin has landed himself a great job. Then, Levin receives a mysterious letter in the mail, and life in the Davis family is about to be anything but normal.

- Lisa A. Tortorello, Author of *My Hero, My Ding*

Brilliant! Project Renovatio is a worthy successor to Allison Maruska's bestselling novel *The Fourth Descendant*. The intrigue in the opening lines grabbed me, and by page two I was completely hooked straight through to the end. I loved the fast pace, loved the amazing characters, and loved the completely gripping plot. A sci-fi mystery and a real page turner you won't want to put down, Project Renovatio is a real winner.

- Dan Alatorre, Author of *The Navigators*

Maruska, master of twists and turns, has done it again: picked a gem from the universe with this subtle, science fiction story. Project Renovatio forces us to question our current reality while fully immersing us in an alternate one. Perfectly smart, uniquely engrossing, and thoroughly entertaining, PR trespasses on common ground to stand on its own as a literary portal to a place that feels unexpectedly a lot like home. Let the games begin.

- John Daryll Winston, Author of *IA: BOSS*

Chapter One

Levin looked away from his computer screen and back to the torn-open envelope on his desk. At first, he'd kept it in a drawer, but he opened the drawer repeatedly to ensure the envelope was still there. He moved it to his desk top for more convenient visual confirmation of its presence.

How could a few papers completely disrupt his focus?

After three more glances, he quit trying to get any additional work done. He removed the papers from the envelope, put them in his wallet, and threw the envelope in the trash. As he shut down his computer, his cell phone pinged.

Rana's name lit the screen, as if she knew he needed to talk to her. The papers in his wallet could change both of their lives.

****

Rana and her mother wandered through the bright gymnasium among a few hundred other people.

Dozens of foldable cardboard displays rested on cafeteria tables arranged in neat rows throughout the space.

They found her sister stationed under a basketball hoop. Standing adjacent to her poster board, Dayla proudly explained her study on length of memory. She'd compared the number of digits different groups of people memorized, an advanced study for a fourth grader. Most of the other kids completed projects on volcanos or tested the theory that plants die when watered with mouthwash.

As they moved towards Dayla's display, stopping along the way to see some of the more interesting projects, Rana's mother typed messages on her phone. She brought her hand to her forehead after a ping. "You have got to be kidding me."

"What?" Rana peered at the phone but couldn't read the message.

"I arranged for someone to cover me on this trip. She didn't show. We have no representation at the conference."

"What does that mean? Do you have to leave again?" Her mother had returned from a two-week trip last week, and she usually had long breaks between work assignments.

She wiggled her thumbs over the screen. "I'm not sure. We're trying to land a big project and networking is important. Let me make a call." She stepped towards the wall as she pressed her phone to her ear.

Listening to the beginning of the conversation, Rana brushed her dark hair from in front of her eyes and scanned the many faces in the room. Her friend was supposed to meet her.

"Rana, over here!" Jacey waved from the open exterior door. Her short, blonde hair shone in the sunlight spilling inside.

"Hey, Jace. How's Brayden's project going? I haven't seen his yet."

"Ugh. He insisted on stuffing Mentos into a bottle of Diet Coke. Like a thousand other kids haven't already done that."

Rana squinted. "Didn't you do that for your fourth grade project?"

"Exactly. Would it kill him to be original? He only had six years to think of a new idea. Too bad he waited until last week to start it."

Rana laughed. "Dayla's worked on hers since January."

Jacey headed for the display on the end of the first row. "Yeah, but you guys aren't normal. I bet she didn't copy your idea, either."

"No, not even close."

"Show off."

The friends wandered through the sea of friendly chatter, studying the projects and asking questions of their creators. Dayla spoke enthusiastically about her project, talking with her hands and arms and nearly hitting Rana in the face.

Her mother found Rana and Jacey next to a project on bug traps. "I need to go to that conference. Not getting that account means layoffs." She pursed her lips.

Rana picked at her nails. "It's okay."

"Jacey's mom will give you a ride home. Love you." She kissed each of her daughters and headed for the exit.

Jacey scrunched her nose. "That stinks. Wanna come over for dinner?"

Rana tapped her fingers against her leg. "No. I'll text Levin to come get us. He'll want to take Dayla out to celebrate her project anyway."

An hour later, Rana and Dayla climbed into their brother's Corolla and headed into town. Dayla beamed. They hardly ever got to eat out.

Levin drove to the 50's style diner Dayla chose. Oldies music mixed with loud conversations and banging dishes filled the place, and the smell of old vegetable oil permeated the air, but Rana didn't complain. Over dinner, Dayla told Levin about the science fair projects, and Rana filled him in on her latest debate team assignment. While the girls did all the talking, Levin sat quietly and tore a straw wrapper into microscopic pieces.

Rana leaned forward and stared at him until his eyes connected with hers. "Something wrong?"

Levin set down the wrapper, pursed his lips, and peered to the far end of the restaurant. "Dayla, why don't you go play that video game?"

Her face lit up.

He pulled quarters from his pocket, handed them to her, and pointed towards the game. She bounded off.

With the two of them remaining, Rana folded her arms on the table and listened to *Rock Around the Clock* while she waited for him to talk.

Levin retrieved his wallet from his pocket, pulled papers from it, and unfolded them. "I got a weird letter in the mail today. From a guy my age who lives in San Diego. He also sent this."

He held the papers and slid a small photograph across the table.

She picked it up. "He sent you a picture of you?"

"Look closer."

She analyzed the picture for a few seconds before spotting what he meant–the subject's nose was too thin. The man's other features–black, wavy hair, dark eyes, olive skin, and medium build–appeared identical to her brother's. "Who is this?"

"His name is Scott. His dad's a reputable scientist who only has a couple more weeks to live. Scott said he went through some paperwork, and he stumbled onto evidence that his dad has a secret, well, 'other' family."

Rana still held the picture but glared at her brother. "What did he find?" *And what does this have to do with us?*

"Old bills, a couple letters, and this." He handed her a paper displaying a color copy of a photograph. "Those kids are me and you. The man is Scott's dad. I was five, and you were one." He leaned towards her. "I think this guy is our dad."

Scowling, Rana studied the man in the picture, who sported dark hair like hers and Levin's. She shook her head. "Our dad died before I was born."

"According to Mom"

"Why would she lie about that?"

"Maybe there was something about him she wanted to keep hidden–like a secret family. I tried to find information about him on the internet and came up empty."

Rana huffed. "I can't believe Mom would hide something this huge from us, especially for so long."

"She does go on a lot of business trips."

"Well, consultants do that." Since her promotion, their mother left town for work assignments with increasing frequency, leaving them in the care of their stepdad, Walt. Before tonight, Rana had no reason to suspect her mother did anything other than what she'd told them. She'd even brought them souvenirs a few times–cheap goodies that vendors handed out at conferences. Rana kept a keychain flashlight bearing the name of a security company next to her bed. If her mother had a secret relationship, she'd gone to great lengths to hide it.

Unable to stomach the idea of her mother leaving them for days or weeks at a time to have an affair, Rana changed the subject. "How'd this guy find you?"

"He used a combination of the old paperwork and the internet. Mom's name occasionally appeared, and she wrote our names in some of the letters. He must have Googled my name and landed on my company's website. He probably included his own picture when he saw mine on the staff page." Levin sipped his soda. "It's not every day you get mail from your doppelganger."

She tapped the table with the edge of the photograph. "So what do we do with this?"

"What do you think about flying to San Diego to check it out?"

She stopped tapping. "Have you talked to Mom?"

"No. I want to see for myself first. You should come with me."

"Are you crazy? I have school. I have a debate tournament next weekend. And what about Dayla?"

"What about her?"

"Well, this obviously doesn't involve her. She's Walt's daughter. And she would hate it if we went on a trip and left her behind."

"What if she isn't Walt's daughter?"

Rana tilted her head and held up the picture. "She looks nothing like this guy."

"She doesn't really look like Walt, either."

"How many secret families do you think Mom has?"

"I'm just saying. If this checks out," he pointed to the photograph, "Dayla might have a secret father, too."

Rana stared at the picture and fidgeted with her black curly hair, which greatly contrasted with Dayla's straight, reddish-brown locks. Dayla's striking green eyes, thin physique, and freckles further differentiated her appearance from those of her siblings. Until now, Rana assumed Dayla inherited her looks from Walt's side of the family. But Levin was right. Aside from her height, Dayla didn't resemble Walt or the relatives they'd met at reunions. If Levin's theory was correct, their father was dying in California, and Dayla's could be out there somewhere.

Before Rana could further consider their parentage, Dayla plopped next to her in the booth. "I ran out of quarters."

Rana passed the picture to Levin and faced her sister. "Levin's taking a trip to California, and he asked me to join him."

Dayla smiled. "Really? Can I come too?"

Levin answered for Rana. "Of course you can."

Chapter Two

They decided to wait until the girls' summer break to go to San Diego. Levin told their mother they'd planned a vacation, and she didn't question it–Levin living on his own and supporting himself by the age of twenty probably told her he could handle his sisters and keep them safe.

That gave Rana three weeks to focus on school and the real reason she joined the debate team.

Jason Burke.

In the three months since debate started, she hadn't mustered the guts to talk to him, though she had done more than her share of nonverbal flirting. She checked her teeth and hair in a window's reflection before heading to the classroom.

She froze in the doorway. He sat in the second row, chatting with another guy and facing the door. He looked at her, and maybe he kept his eyes on her a little longer than he did yesterday. Her pulse quickened.

Someone shoved her from behind, and she continued into the room. She claimed the seat directly in front of Jason–better for him to stare at the back of her head than to let him see the stupid grin on her face. She regretted the decision immediately, though, because she couldn't see if he had a stupid grin on his face from her position.

She felt silly for joining the debate team for a boy, especially one she intentionally blocked from her vision. With nothing to do while she waited for the teacher to arrive, she scribbled on her notebook cover. Sensing motion to her right, she looked up. Jason took the seat next to her.

"Hi. I prefer the front row, don't you?" He smiled at her. Her eyes shifted between his freckled cheeks and spiky, reddish-brown hair.

"Um . . . sure." Heat rushed to her face and she examined her notebook, as if that would keep him from noticing her pale cheeks turning the color of a maraschino cherry.

Sitting sideways in his seat, he placed one elbow on the chair and the other on the desk, clasping his hands in front of him. "So, I thought you had a really solid argument against the use of GMOs last week. Am I allowed to say that, since I argued the opposing side?"

She anxiously laughed. "Yeah. You were great, too." Why did all her words sound dumb?

He looked towards her desk. "Anyway, I was wondering, since we only have a few more weeks of school and I'm running out of time to ask, if you want to get together for a movie or something." His eyes made their way back to hers.

She sat with her mouth agape for a moment before shaking off the shock. “Yeah, that sounds great!”

“Good.” He exhaled, and his shoulders dropped. “I’m going to a bunch of graduation parties until the end of the year, but maybe after school’s out?”

“Um, okay. I’m going to San Diego with my brother and sister, but only for a week.”

“Oh, all right. Do you have your phone on you? I’ll give you my number.”

She nodded, retrieved her phone from her backpack, and added his number to her contact list as he recited it.

“Just give me a call when you get back, okay?”

“Okay. Thanks.” She gazed into his eyes.

She snapped out of her trance when the teacher entered the room and assigned positions for the next tournament, but she hardly heard what he said. She resisted the urge to glance at Jason’s number on her phone.

****

Levin took Maggie’s hand as they walked through the park. The sun lowering behind the Colorado Rockies gave everything around them a magical glow, including the red highlights in Maggie’s brown hair. He couldn’t take his gaze away from her.

Maggie grinned at him. “I’m glad it’s finally warm enough to walk around outside. This would have been a little cold on our first date.”

“Yeah, Valentine’s Day was a bit chilly. Although it would have given me an excuse to hold you right away.”

She laughed. “Are you ready for your trip?”

"I think so." He looked towards the path and put his other hand in his pocket.

"Is something wrong?"

The anxiety he'd tried to ignore rushed to the front of his mind. He took a deep breath to push it back, but it became harder to suppress as the trip neared. "Do you remember I told you I never knew my biological father?"

She squinted. "Yeah, I remember."

"My mom always told me and Rana that he died in a car accident when I was three. Mom was pregnant with Rana at the time. I don't remember him at all. Anyway, I got a letter in the mail a few weeks ago. The guy who sent it said his dad might have a secret family, and we're that family. That's why we're going to California."

"Really?" She paused, as if deciding for herself what to do with the information. "Do you think it's true?"

"I hope not. I don't want to talk to my mom about it." He kept her hand in his but stared at his feet and kicked the rocks on the path.

She pulled on his arm, stopping their forward motion, and faced him. "Why don't you want to talk to her?"

He looked over her head towards a group playing Frisbee as he considered his answer.

"I've never . . . I don't like confrontation. And asking why she lied to us our whole lives would require a pretty big confrontation. My family is happy. I'm close with my sisters. Our stepdad does his own thing. We're . . . comfortable, I guess."

She wrapped her arms around him and rested her head on his chest. “You got the letter a few weeks ago?”

“Yeah.”

“Why didn’t you tell me about it then?”

He stroked her hair. “I wasn’t sure how you would react. Whenever things got serious with other girls, it ended. And this is way more serious than anything that happened with them.” He pulled back enough to gaze into her eyes and sighed. “I kinda like having you around.”

She kept her eyes locked on his. “You won’t get rid of me that easily.”

Relief covered him. He leaned over, kissed her, and pulled her into his arms.

Chapter Three

Eight hours after leaving Denver, Levin drove towards the setting sun while his mind kept returning to his date with Maggie. The late afternoon light had brightened her hair and skin, and her laugh echoed in his memory. Instead of his story scaring her away, she'd drawn closer to him. The more he dwelled on her, the more the truth insisted on occupying his attention: he loved her.

He allowed the euphoria to course through him, as he hadn't come anywhere close to this with other girls. His status as a soccer player might have helped his dating situation in high school, but his awkward computer geek status canceled out any benefits his athleticism offered. He'd taken his cousin to the prom.

Considering how much his life had changed, he couldn't suppress his smile.

"Okay, what's going on with you? You've been super quiet and randomly smiling since we left." Rana lowered her tablet to her lap and cornered him from the passenger seat.

He tried to think of a way to explain himself. Aware his relationship would present a source of incessant teasing, he hadn't told his sisters about Maggie. But Rana busted him, and they still had nine hours of road trip before reaching San Diego.

"Well, are you gonna tell us or not?" Dayla asked from the back seat.

"Oh, I get a choice? I choose not."

Rana smacked him on the shoulder. "Don't be like that. Is it about a girl?"

"What? Come on." His stubborn smile betrayed the surprise he tried to fake.

"Oh my gosh, it is," squealed Dayla. "Out with it!"

He expressed an exaggerated sigh. "Fine. You win. Her name is Maggie. Happy now?"

"No," the girls said unanimously.

He kept both hands on the wheel and his eyes straight ahead. "We met four months ago. A friend set us up."

"Four months. That beats your old record by . . . what? Three months?" Rana asked.

He looked away from the road long enough to glare at her. "Yeah. Anyway, I really like her. She's beautiful and smarter than I can imagine. She's finishing her biology degree and going to medical school after that."

He smiled again as his heart raced. How had he attracted such an amazing girl?

Dayla bounced in her seat. "Can we meet her?"

"I wasn't even going to tell you about her. One step at a time, okay?"

Adrenaline raced through him when he imagined introducing Maggie to his sisters. In his mind, she naturally fit with his family, like she belonged in it.

The thought gave him enough energy to run to San Diego. “How about I drive through the night? Then we’ll get there by morning.”

Rana nodded, and Dayla added, “I bet Maggie’s really pretty.”

He smiled again. Rana laughed.

****

They arrived in San Diego early the next morning. After a fast food breakfast and plenty of coffee for Levin, they found a health club with public access and showers.

Rana left Dayla to finish showering and wandered to the front of the building, where she’d arranged to meet Levin. He pulled his phone away from his ear and pocketed it.

“Did you call Scott?”

He nodded. “He’ll text the address. We’re meeting in a couple hours.”

“Are you nervous?”

He shrugged. “A little. Are you?”

Rana’s nerves crowded her stomach so much she’d had to force herself to eat her breakfast sandwich. “Yeah. It’s pretty huge. We might meet our real dad.”

He blinked a few times. “Okay, now I’m nervous. Thanks for that.”

She laughed. “You haven’t thought about it?”

“Yeah, I’ve thought about it. I just...” He peered over her head. “I guess I got used to the idea of not having a father, you know?”

Rana's throat tightened. Though their mother had married Walt around the time Dayla was born, he was frequently deployed for many of their early years as a family, and after his discharge he hid away in his bedroom or office, rarely interacting with them. The situation had brought her and her siblings closer over the years. Her mother often said Levin grew up quickly, acting like a father towards his sisters at times. Their relationship was unusual, but Rana had no desire to change it.

Levin's phone rang. He pulled it from his pocket and grinned when he looked at the screen. "I'm gonna take this. Why don't you check on Dayla?" He put the phone to his ear and walked outside.

Rana and Dayla met him at the car a few minutes later. They piled in, and Dayla leaned forward, putting her head between the front seats. "Can we go to the zoo today?"

Levin started the engine. "Not today. I have an appointment."

"An appointment? We're on vacation."

"I know. An old friend wanted to get together. It won't take all day."

Dayla scowled, fell back into her seat, and opened her book featuring a variety of African animals on the cover. "I wanted to finish this before we went anyway."

Levin referenced his phone and punched the address Scott sent into his GPS.

His address. The guy who could be my brother. Rana took a breath to settle her nerves as Levin turned right onto a busy street.

Levin drove for thirty minutes, and they looked for a house with numbers matching those Scott gave them. They soon left the residential area and drove into an industrial one.

Rana scowled. “That’s weird. I thought we were meeting Scott at a house.”

“So did I, but I guess he didn’t actually say that.” Levin picked up the GPS and examined it.

“Why are you meeting him, Rana? Isn’t this Levin’s appointment?” Dayla asked.

Rana’s eyes widened, and she mentally kicked herself for blowing their cover story. She tried to recover. “You’re right. It is. But he’s not meeting a friend. It’s about…”

“It’s about our dad,” Levin said.

“Dad? You mean Walt?”

“No.” He waved his finger between Rana and himself. “I mean *our* dad.”

“But he died.”

Rana sighed. “There might be more to the story. No more questions for now.”

“But–”

“I mean it.”

“Fine.” Dayla fell back into the seat.

The address belonged to a large, clean office building. A guard sat in a booth next to a gate that closed off the parking lot. He grabbed a clipboard and left the booth as Levin pulled up. Levin lowered his window.

“Can I help you?” The guard glared through the window.

Levin blinked a few times. “Uh . . . yeah. I’m Levin Davis, and I have an appointment with Scott Miles.”

The guard referenced the clipboard. “Mr. Miles canceled your meeting. Go back the way you came.” He re-entered his booth before Levin could ask him to elaborate.

Levin scowled at the guard and put the car in reverse. He pointed it towards the houses.

“Now what do we do?” Rana asked.

“Good question. I’ll call Scott when we stop somewhere and find out what happened.”

After Levin drove through the neighborhood and reached the commercial area where they’d started their day, Dayla asked, “Where are we going now?”

“I’m not sure.” He stopped at a red light. A man wearing dirt-covered clothes stood on the corner. His beard reached his chest, and he held a cardboard sign asking for money. He glanced at Rana, pulled a paper from his pocket, and walked towards her window.

She tensed as he approached. The man tapped on the window and motioned for her to open it while showing her the paper, which had Levin’s name written on it. She looked at Levin. He nodded.

Rana lowered the window an inch. The man slipped the paper through the gap, saluted them casually, and returned to his corner.

She unfolded the paper and read another address. Levin entered into his GPS. Ten minutes later, Levin pulled into the parking lot of a small coffee shop.

“Levin, what’s going on?” Rana asked. Following strangers to random addresses couldn’t be a smart move.

"I don't know. Wait here. I'll check it out."

****

Levin left the girls in the car and entered the coffee shop. He scanned the place for any patrons who looked like him; an old lady drinking tea and a young Hispanic guy typing on a laptop comprised the shop's current customer population. Unsure of why he was here, Levin approached the counter and ordered a double shot cappuccino. He read the fliers on the wall while the barista prepared it.

Scott must have paid the homeless guy to give them the address–a strange way to communicate, but maybe Scott liked to play with people. Levin assumed Scott changed the location and had expected to find him sitting at a table when he arrived. Should he wait for Scott to join him?

As the barista handed him his drink, she asked, "Is your name Levin?"

He stepped back. "Uh, who wants to know?"

She leaned over the counter. "A guy came in here earlier. Said another guy who looks like him would come in. He told me to give you this. Paid me twenty dollars. Said he would come back for the money if you didn't get it. I really need the money, so here."

She handed him a small, sealed envelope with something solid and rectangular inside.

He scrunched his eyebrows. "Okay, thanks." He took the envelope and his coffee and returned to the car.

Rana glared at him with wide eyes.

He set his coffee in the cup holder and tore open the envelope. He reached inside and removed a thumb drive.

"Where did you get that?" Rana asked.

"Scott paid the barista to give it to me." He yanked his phone from his pocket. "Time to find out what the hell's going on."

He pressed Scott's name in his recent contact lists. A recorded message saying the number was no longer in service answered back.

He ended the call. "I guess we're on our own."

Chapter Four

Levin booked a two-star hotel room for five nights, glad to finally accomplish something. Dayla claimed one side of the bed she and Rana would share, set a pillow against the headboard, and cracked open a book about animals native to Asia. She had finished the one featuring African animals in the car while they traveled around the city.

Levin and Rana sat at the table by the window. He pulled the laptop from his backpack, set it on the table, and twisted around to face Dayla. “Rana and I need to work on the computer. We’ll get lunch when we’re done. Okay?”

“Yep.” She quickly immersed herself in the world of the Chinese red panda.

Levin inserted the thumb drive. It stored a single file. He opened the file as his breath caught in his chest. *What if this crashes my system?* Too late now.

The screen displayed an article written in 1991.

"He paid the barista to give us a twenty-two-year-old article?" Rana asked.

"Apparently."

They read the text silently. It described the research behind genetically modified organisms and how their use could increase the global food supply. A company engineered a tomato with a longer shelf life. Levin skimmed to the end, where the last paragraph caught his attention.

> *As scientists pave the way for genetically engineered food to enter the country's–and indeed, the world's–food supply, it is no great leap to assume that one day, genetically engineered humans will walk among us.*

What did any of this have to do with the reason they came? And why the covert operation to give him the file?

Rana interrupted his thoughts. "We debated GMO use at one of our tournaments. It's so much worse now than when this came out. That part about genetically altered humans is ridiculous, though."

"Why?"

"Well," she looked at the ceiling, "in the case of genetic engineering on produce, scientists insert a Bt gene into the crop DNA that kills insects if they eat it. Or they can insert a bacterial gene that makes the crops resistant to herbicides. People ingest the foods with these genes in them, and no one knows the long term health effects of that."

"Okay." Levin watched as Rana appeared to make connections in her head.

"And I doubt anyone would combine human DNA with other genes like that. Being genetically resistant to mosquitoes would be nice, though." She laughed. "I guess someone could *mutate* human genes. I don't know." She faced him. "What does this have to do with why we're here?"

He shrugged. "Let's see what we can search."

They both scanned the article.

"How about the author? Patrice Jevon Root," she said.

"Worth a shot."

He typed the name into a search engine. Nothing. Strange, considering the vast majority of people had at least *something* about them on the internet. He searched for information on the genetically modified tomato and found only generic facts.

Leaning back in the chair, he put his hands over his face and groaned. "Well, I'm stumped. Let's go to the zoo. Seems we've got nothing better to do. Maybe we'll think of something while we're out."

Dayla leapt off the bed. "Yay!"

****

Dayla skipped ahead of Rana as they walked towards the entrance, rattling off the information she had absorbed from her books since they left home. "Did you know the Nile Crocodile can weigh 11,000 pounds? And you can hear a lion's roar from five miles away? I read today that a red panda is solitary. I like it because I like to be alone too..." She tended to become a resident expert on any exhibits their mother took them to, which over the years had grown into a significant number.

"That's great, hon. Which animal do you want to see now?" Rana became overwhelmed at the mass of information Dayla threw at her and needed a distraction. She handed Dayla the map. Levin seemed content to stare into the crowd through his sunglasses.

Dayla pointed to the map. "Let's see the orangutan. Do you know most people say it wrong? It's orangu-tan, not orangu-tang. I feel bad for it because no one can say its name. Like you, Rana. It's Ray-na, not Rah-na. Do you think it knows no one can say its name? I think it does. Hey! The orangutan is a loner too. Just like the red panda…"

Rana semi-quit listening as Dayla skipped along, happy to be a living library of zoo facts. She pitied any docent who presented incorrect information in front of the child.

They spent the following hours visiting the exhibits Dayla chose. She spouted off information at each one and even drew a little crowd.

Rana put her hand on her sister's shoulder and bent down to meet her eyes. "Look, it's great you know so much, but tell us your two or three favorite facts for each animal so we don't attract attention."

"Okay, I guess." Dayla sulked and glanced at the sign near the elephant exhibit. "Hey, that's not right."

Levin stepped next to her. "What?"

"This map on the sign says African elephants live in northwest Africa. That's wrong. They live in central and southern Africa. Geez, that's so easy to learn. Should I tell someone?"

"No, stay here. I'll mention it on the way out." Levin leaned towards the sign and picked at it.

"What are you doing?" Rana asked.

"The corner doesn't line up. Something's under it." He continued to pick and tug at it.

Rana moved next to Levin, hoping to block him from anyone else's view. Dayla wouldn't appreciate their zoo trip ending with employees kicking them out for vandalizing their sign. Fortunately, no one else seemed interested.

"There." Levin lifted the sign, revealing another sign with a map showing the correct distribution of African elephants. He examined the fake sign.

"Someone left a note on the back." He read it and groaned.

"Can I see it?" Rana asked, and Levin handed it to her. She read:

Congratulations on finding a well-buried clue. Perhaps you'd like to search for me again? Meet me at the burger place on the corner of Columbia and Grape Street in thirty minutes.

Patrice Jevon Root

She lowered the sign. Levin was walking towards the fence separating the zoo from the outside world.

She caught up to him. "Do you want to go?"

"No, I want to see who's watching us. Someone must be close enough to tell whoever left the message that we found it." He took off his sunglasses and squinted as he studied the landscape.

Rana tried to think of a plan. "Let's just go to the restaurant. You can find out who left it when we get there."

He glared at her. "Doesn't this seem weird to you? Who's interested enough in our lives to lead us around? Someone's screwing with us." He paused, as if gathering his thoughts, then turned and rushed towards the exit.

Rana grabbed Dayla's hand and followed.

Chapter Five

As he drove to the restaurant, Levin rubbed his neck. How long had someone been watching him and his sisters? Since home? Since they arrived in San Diego? His stomach sank again when he mentally reread the note. They knew what he searched on his laptop. He'd been careless to use a public wifi network, and now whoever tracked him had the upper hand.

Swallowing the lump in his throat, he pressed the accelerator, determined to discover who invaded his privacy.

He found the place with five minutes to spare and faced his sisters. "Stay in the car. If everything inside looks legit, I'll wave you in."

They nodded.

As he approached the door, he drummed his fingers on his leg, and when he reached for the handle, he hesitated.

What if these people were dangerous?

This is a public place. Whoever this is won't try anything here.

He took a reassuring breath and pulled the door open.

Poking his head inside, he took off his sunglasses and looked around. A small bar and several tables and booths filled the interior, and generic pop music played through the speakers. Patrons filled half of the space; he recognized one of them.

He waved the girls to the front door. "Scott's in a booth near the kitchen. I want you two to sit at a different table." He scanned the interior again. "Go sit at the empty one by the window so I can see you." He gave them money for their food. They walked to their table, and he headed towards the booth.

Scott rose to greet him. "Levin. You must have received my note." He shook Levin's hand with a firm grip and smiled widely.

"*Your* note? Should I call you Patrice?"

Scott laughed. "Please, take a seat. The girls are welcome to join us. I'm paying for everyone's meals either way."

"I can cover our own food." Levin scowled. "And I prefer to keep our conversation between the two of us."

"Suit yourself."

A waitress with frizzy hair and a frown approached, and the men placed their orders. Scott instructed her to include Rana and Dayla on his bill.

Levin's jaw dropped, and he started to restate his position but sat back. It wasn't worth the argument, and he had bigger issues at hand.

"Well, Levin, it's nice to finally meet you. If you don't mind my asking, how did your mom choose your name? It's one of the more unusual ones I've heard."

"Oh, well, my mom wanted to name me after her grandpa, but his first name was Otis. She worried I'd get picked on, so she gave me his last name for my first name."

Scott nodded. "I see. And how do you like it?"

"I still got picked on, but it's fine now." He sat back and crossed his arms, ready to cut the small talk. "How long have you been watching us? I don't appreciate being followed."

Scott must have realized Levin's serious tone and responded in kind. "We've had our eyes on you since you arrived in San Diego and not before, I assure you."

"Why? Why all the sneaking around and secret thumb drives and paying off baristas and hidden messages under signs? We could've met for breakfast and saved a whole day."

"That was a bit of a test. We know of the high intelligence of you and your sisters, and we wanted to see how much you could figure out on your own."

"We didn't figure out that much. The article meant nothing, and Dayla noticed the map. That's it. And how would you know about our 'high intelligence'?"

Scott folded his arms on the table and leaned forward. "Let me guess: you graduated high school at sixteen or seventeen with half of your college credits already earned, went straight into a Bachelor's program, and graduated by nineteen. What kind of scholarship did you receive? Sports?"

Levin glared at him, not wanting to give him the satisfaction of being right. "Soccer." He squinted at

Scott for another moment. "How do you know all that?"

Scott held solid eye contact with Levin. "I'm not here to answer all of your questions, but to perhaps point you in the right direction. You recall what the article described?"

"Yeah, it was about genetic engineering in produce. So?"

"At the end, it described the possibility of altering DNA in humans. What did you think of that?"

"I don't know much about genetics. Rana's studied the topic, and she said it's ridiculous. I believe her."

Scott shook his head. "We've made greater strides in genetic manipulation than anyone knows about."

"What's that supposed to mean? And who is this 'we' you keep referring to?" Levin rubbed his forehead and scanned the restaurant for the waitress. Maybe it wasn't too late to order another coffee.

Scott leaned into the table and clasped his hands in front of him. "My father lives in Greece. I haven't met him. Scientists chose him as a genetic donor for a government operation called Project Renovatio."

Levin held up a hand. "Project what-a-who-vio?"

Scott laughed. "Renovatio. That's Latin for 'renewal.' Anyway, the scientists modified the genetic structure of his and my mother's cells to enhance characteristics in their child that would increase the chance of survival in an . . . unstable environment. One subject to severe effects of climate change or cataclysmic war." He stopped, as if waiting for a response.

"Okay, I'll bite. What characteristics?"

"Increased intelligence, high physical endurance, and stronger immunity, for example."

Levin stared at Scott. "You're telling me you're a genetically modified human?"

"Basically, yes. I and those like me would rebuild society and start to renew the human population, if necessary."

"Okay." Levin looked towards his sisters and shook his head. What a waste of time.

"I can tell you're dismissing my claim. That's fine. But I encourage you to continue looking into the matter yourself. In fact, you should speak to your mother."

"My mother? What makes you think she knows anything?"

"Don't you remember the letter I mailed to you? About the secret family? That wasn't just a lure to get you here."

"All right, I'm done." Levin put his palms on the table and lifted himself from the booth. He stood, facing Scott. "Thanks for the dinner. I hope you don't mind if I spend the rest of the evening with my sisters. I appreciate your time and your . . . information."

"Of course not. I hope you enjoy your time here." He stood and shook Levin's hand. "You won't hear from us again for the rest of your trip."

"Good."

Levin started approaching his sisters, paused, and turned back. "Who is Patrice Jevon Root?"

Scott grinned. "You should ask Dayla that question."

Levin scrunched his eyebrows and walked to his sisters' table. He sat next to Rana and looked at Scott's booth–Scott had left his table and stopped a waitress, apparently to pay for their meals, before he exited the restaurant. At least the guy stuck to his word.

"So? What did he say?" Rana asked.

"He's a whack job." Levin told his sisters what Scott said about Project Renovatio, his Greek father, and the modified genes.

Dayla piped in. "Project Renovatio? How do you spell that?"

Levin spelled it, and she used a crayon to write it on her kids' menu. She drew arrows from the letters and wrote them in different orders.

As they finished eating, the waitress approached their table and pointed to the front door. "Was that guy your twin?"

Levin shook his head.

"You guys should get an act going in Vegas." She chuckled and held a card displaying a scrawled phone number out to him. "He asked me to give you this. I wondered why you didn't have your twin's number." She laughed again as she walked to another table.

Rana sipped her soda and leaned towards him, studying the card. "Looks like the games continue."

"Yeah." He slipped the card into his wallet.

"Aren't you gonna call?"

"No. I'm tired of people lying to me."

"What did he say about the picture?"

"I didn't ask." He yanked his keys from his pocket. "Let's go. I'm done dealing with this."

"Hold on!" Dayla wrote two last letters on her menu and held it up for her siblings to see. "It's an anagram." She beamed. Her arrows and letter combinations transformed *Project Renovatio* into *Patrice Jevon Root*.

Okay, so Scott wasn't completely nuts.

****

Levin's voice boomed through the bathroom door. "Are you coming or not?"

"Yeah, give me a minute." Wearing her bathing suit, Rana stood in the middle of the bathroom, ready to go swimming with her siblings. But first, she needed time alone in the hotel room. "Why don't you take Dayla? I'll meet you there when I'm ready."

"Well, are you close?"

"Not really."

"All right. But try to finish before we drive home in two days."

"Ha ha."

The door to their room slammed shut. Rana crept out of the bathroom, found Levin's shorts draped on the bed, and yanked his wallet from the pocket. She retrieved the card, nervously dialed the numbers into her phone, and waited.

Levin had said he didn't want to deal with Scott any longer, but if he meant it, why did he keep the phone number? She didn't have the answers she'd wanted when they arrived in California, and if Levin wouldn't look for them, she had to.

"Hello?"

"Hi, um, is this Scott?"

"Yes, who's this?"

She swallowed her anxiety. "Rana Davis. You met with my brother the other night at that burger place."

"Of course. How is your trip going?"

“Fine. Listen, I don’t have much time. I want to ask you about your dad.”

“Okay. What do you want to know?”

“The truth. The man in the picture you sent to Levin isn’t your father, but you suggested he was.”

“Did I? I just sent the picture with the information that my dad had another family.”

Rana stood in silence for a moment. “Okay, so why did you send it?”

“I knew you would make that inference, and I needed you–well, just Levin, really–to come to San Diego to meet me.”

“Why? What did you tell him that you couldn’t say over the phone?”

He sighed. “I appreciate your curiosity, but I can’t give you any more information than I already gave to Levin. As I told him, you should talk to your mother. Thank you for calling me.” The call ended.

Rana looked at the card. Levin hadn’t said anything to her about Scott telling him to talk to their mother. Why would he omit that piece of the conversation?

She replaced the card and Levin’s wallet and left the room.

Chapter Six

After another overnight drive, Levin parked the car in his mother's driveway. Walt sat at the patio table on the porch with his laptop, occasionally looking at the sprinkler that watered the dirt patch he liked to call the front yard. His dirty, sleeveless biker shirt, denim cutoffs, and overgrown dirty blond hair greatly contrasted with his sleek computer. He glanced at the car before returning his focus to the screen.

Levin exited the car with the girls, and for the first time in his life, he dreaded speaking to his mother. While he'd hoped to disregard everything Scott had said, Scott's knowledge of Dayla's puzzle-solving skills made ignoring him impossible. Whether Levin liked it or not, he had to confront his mother if he wanted to know the truth.

Liz stood on the porch as her children approached her. Her long, brown hair pulled into a ponytail made her appear significantly younger than her forty-five years. She hugged each of them when they reached her. A wide smile covered most of her thin face.

"Welcome home! I missed you so much. So, tell me everything." She had some knowledge of their San Diego activities, as Rana called her to check in nearly every night. She trusted Levin with his sisters, but the protective parent in her demanded frequent updates.

The four entered the living room. The girls sat with their mother on the faux leather sofa in front of the window while Levin reclined in the neighboring chair. Nineties pop music played from the stereo in the kitchen.

Dayla bounced on the cushion. "It was awesome. Levin had a meeting the first morning, but it was canceled. Someone gave him an article that he read on his computer. Then, we went to the zoo. The map on the sign by the African elephants was wrong. Then, we went to a burger place. I sat with Rana because Levin met with a guy named Scott. I ordered a cheeseburger and tater tots. I figured out an anagram. I love anagrams. The words were Project Renovatio, which was an anagram for Patrice Jovan Root, who wrote the article that Levin read on his computer. Weird. Then, the next day, we went back to the zoo…"

Liz glared at him when Dayla said "Project Renovatio," challenging his hope that she didn't know anything about it. The anxiety in his gut increased, and he shifted in his seat.

Dayla finished her play-by-play of their vacation, and Levin needed his sisters to leave before talking to his mother about the real reason for their trip.

"Dayla, why don't you go upstairs and take a bath?" He scrunched his nose. "You need one."

"Very funny." She hugged her mom one more time before retreating up the stairs.

He watched her leave and faced Rana. "I need to talk to Mom. Can you go unpack?"

"It's okay. I know Scott told you to talk to her. I called him the night you took Dayla to the pool."

Levin sat with his mouth open for a moment. "What? Why would you–"

"He wouldn't leave all those clues for us and then let the trail go cold. I wanted to know what you didn't tell me, so I called him." Her matter-of-fact yet strong tone dared him to call her out on her intrusion.

For a second he clenched his jaw and considered demanding she leave. He rarely fought with anyone in his family–or anyone not in his family, for that matter. His inexperience resulted in his current speechlessness.

She broke his silence. "I can handle it. Really. I want to stay."

He dreaded discussing the subject with Rana there, but his mother watched him as if waiting for him to ask, apparently unconcerned with Rana's presence.

"Fine." He faced Liz. "So what do you know about Project Renovatio? Scott told me I should ask you. He said you could tell us about our father."

Her shoulders dropped. "I suspected this had something to do with why you went to San Diego. Wait here."

She left the couch and walked up the stairs. Levin and Rana stared at each other while the musical workings of Smash Mouth intruded on their serious moods. Before returning to the couch, Liz entered the kitchen and turned off the music.

She held a thin book with a blue cover, which she set on the coffee table in front of the couch and opened to the first page. It displayed a yellow flier.

"When I was twenty-three years old, I moved to San Diego to live with my boyfriend. The relationship fell apart soon after I arrived. I needed to move out of his apartment, but I didn't have a place to go, and I only worked a part time job at a hotel. I couldn't find a job that fit my degree. I moved in with some roommates because the rent was cheap, but they were slobs. I had to find my own place. One day, I saw this flier on an announcement board of a college campus I walked through on my way to work." She turned the book around so Levin could read the flier.

> *Need extra money? An organization seeks individuals to participate in a research study. We will assess your qualifications for inclusion in the study. All subjects will receive $100 for answering this ad, whether or not they qualify. Those who qualify will be eligible for additional compensation.*

"I was desperate for money, so I called the number. I went to an office building outside of town. Techs had me complete surveys, take IQ and fitness tests, and they drew some blood. After they finished screening me, a man named Dr. Steven Craig met with me privately." She turned the page of the scrapbook. It displayed a business card for Dr. Craig: Geneticist. The man pictured on the card looked familiar. Levin's eyes moved to a piece of paper with small print that his mother had signed.

"He said I had qualities his research team sought for their project. He called it Project Renovatio. His team wanted to collect the reproductive cells of individuals with above average intelligence, language skills, strength, endurance, or immunity, modify their genetic structure, and combine them to create offspring who would fully express their desired qualities. The children could survive in a harsh environment. I qualified because I scored well on the IQ test, and the blood test indicated I had a strong immune system. He offered me a yearly compensation of twenty thousand dollars to sign this contract saying I would participate in the Project–meaning I would carry and raise two children created from my eggs." She turned the page. It showed several sonogram pictures, highlighting different stages of a developing fetus.

Rana glared at her mother. "How could you do that? You . . . signed your life over to a research organization."

Liz traced one of the pictures with her finger. "I needed the money, but also because I had a chance to make a significant impact on history. Human beings could re-create their society should something catastrophic happen to destroy it. My children would be important parts of that, meaning I would also be an important part of it."

"But did you want to have kids by yourself? It sounds to me like they took advantage of women in need."

"I made the choice, Rana." Her mother scowled. "No one forced me to do anything. I wanted to have kids since I was little. I'd like to think you of all people wouldn't argue with my decision."

Rana stared, apparently out of words.

Liz turned back to Levin and gestured to the sonogram images. "These are my first pictures of you. Your father lives in Greece. The Project chose him for his high IQ and superior strength and physical endurance." She turned the page again, showing pictures of Levin as a baby.

"He lives in Greece? You never met him?"

She shook her head. "That was a condition of the agreement. The genetic parents were not to try contacting each other."

"And you agreed to that?" Levin sprung to his feet, paced, and held his hand towards the album. "You were having kids with this guy!"

She followed his motion. "It's like any woman who uses a sperm bank or blind adoption to start families. It's not unheard of."

"How many other kids does he have because of the Project? Do you even know?" He ran his hand through his hair.

"Levin, sit down. Please. I can't talk to you when you're walking back and forth like that."

He sat and clenched his fist. His fingernails dug into his palm.

His mother turned her body, facing him. "To answer your question, I don't know if he had other kids. I suppose he did, though. It wouldn't be economical for them to track down new fathers for each family."

Levin shifted in his seat as he recalled his conversation with Scott, who apparently was his half-brother. How many other half-siblings were they hiding from him? A foul taste developed in the back of his throat.

Turning the pages of the scrapbook, Liz revealed Rana's sonogram and newborn pictures. "You and Rana have the same father. I thought I wouldn't carry any more children for the Project. But they contacted me again five years later saying my genetics complemented those of another male donor especially well, and they offered me an additional ten thousand dollars per year to carry and raise another child. A year later, I gave birth to Dayla. Her father is a Scottish man chosen for his superior language skills and memory."

The scrapbook ended with baby pictures of Dayla.

He kept his eyes on the page. "So we were born because someone paid you to have us."

"In a manner of speaking, yes. Can you not accept that? Every day, infertile couples hire surrogates to carry their children. In a way, that's what I was. A surrogate. Although I carried my own children."

He didn't look at her or say anything. How could she spend two decades hiding the truth about her own children's existence, as if it were an insignificant detail?

"I want you to know," she scooted on the couch towards his chair, "that I believe I was destined to be your mother. I made sure you all had the best chance at developing fully into your genetic makeup. I enrolled you and Rana into sports so you could develop your endurance, I taught Dayla to read at a young age, you all took advanced classes at school, and we traveled to museums all over the country. I wanted to expose you to as many ideas as possible, to make sure you directly benefitted from the money I received from the Project. I hope you can appreciate that."

"Then why tell us all that BS about the accident killing our dad? And why did you marry Walt? We did fine on our own."

She glared. "I married Walt because I loved him." She leaned back into the sofa cushion. "I didn't want to tell you the truth of your existence until all three of you were old enough to accept it. The accident story kept you from asking questions."

"Does Walt know Dayla's not his daughter?"

"Of course he does. He knows all about the Project. We met a couple of months before Dayla was conceived. A few months after that, I suspected the Project was watching me more closely than they said. Walt said he'd stick close by, to protect all of us."

Protect? Levin eyed the sloppy man sitting on the porch.

Liz followed his gaze. "He's had a hard time adjusting to normal life since his discharge. Anyway, he and I fell in love and got married. He wanted to help raise all of you."

Levin leaned forward in his chair. "What do you mean you suspected the Project was watching too closely?"

She sat back and crossed her arms. "I just had a sense that something was off–like I'd get a call from your pediatrician's office reminding me to schedule your appointment, and a week later, in an update letter the Project sent to the moms, they'd say something about making sure to keep up with your wellness checkups. It might have been a coincidence."

"But what if it wasn't?" Levin retrieved the picture from his wallet and handed it to his mother. "Who is that guy?"

She held the picture but didn't look at it. "You grew up without knowing about the Project. I'd say that means they aren't a threat, or Walt and I would have done something about it." She glanced at the picture. "This is Dr. Craig. I took this picture on our last day in San Diego." She turned the scrapbook back to the page with the business card on it. In the picture on the card, Dr. Craig appeared cleaner and more professional than in the photograph, in which he had a thin beard and wore jeans and a T-shirt. "Don't you remember living there, Levin?"

"Not really."

"That's too bad. You loved it." She flipped the pages to the baby pictures.

"Okay, Mom. I'm tired, and I'd like to go home. I'll call you later." He rose from his chair and walked out the front door, leaving her and his sister sitting together on the couch.

****

After a shower and a short nap, Levin invited Maggie to his apartment. She arrived carrying an order of Chinese takeout. He took the food from her, set it on the table, and kissed her. "You're just what I needed to see tonight."

She laughed. "Thanks. I think." She opened the paper bag, releasing the aroma of sesame chicken and cabbage egg rolls. "How was your trip?"

"Educational."

As they ate their meal around his small dining room table, he told her about meeting Scott, and he eased into revealing what his mother said about Project Renovatio.

"So what do you think?" she asked.

He shrugged. "It's ridiculous, but I can't figure out why anyone would make all this up. It all seems really unlikely."

"Why?"

"Come on. A group of researchers alters human DNA to create their own brand of people? It's crazy. It's right out of a science fiction novel. And it makes me one of those genetically altered mutants." He took a bite. "Do you think I have super powers?"

She laughed. "We should explore that. But really, it's not as crazy as you think. Like the old article he gave you–back then, genetically engineered food as we know it was a new idea. Nowadays, people eat genetically modified food all the time. This food probably has genetically modified ingredients. It's not a far reach to suggest someone would do that to human genetics. The rationale even makes sense. Climate change negatively impacts our environment, and foreign enemies seem to always rattle their sabers at us. Maybe we'll need a group of hardy humans."

He considered her point as he used his fork to slide food around his plate. "I don't know."

The email alert pinged on Levin's laptop.

"Do you mind if I check that? I have to go back to work tomorrow. I might need to prepare something."

She shook her head, and he carried his plate to his desk. An email from a new contact had appeared.

Levin stared at Scott's name. "What the hell?"

Maggie joined him at the computer.

"He must have gotten my email address from the company webpage. I thought I was done with him." He opened the message. It contained a video link with a brief description:

Levin, I hoped you would have called me by now, but since you haven't, I've decided to share more information with you this way.

Levin double checked his anti-virus and anti-spyware programs, and he opened the video. It showed Scott sitting in a chair in front of a black backdrop.

"Wow, he looks just like you," Maggie said.

"Yeah. What's with this guy? Is he allergic to talking to people without being all mysterious?"

Levin pressed play, and Scott began speaking. "I apologize for interrupting your evening. I'm aware you've spoken to your mother, and you've probably figured that we are, in fact, half-brothers."

How did Scott know he had talked to his mother? Levin clenched his jaw.

"The creators of PR designed it in a series of phases. Every two years, they collected reproductive cells from the Project's participants, then modified, joined, and placed them into the mothers. Each phase would result in fifty offspring–twenty-five males and twenty-five females. Ten male and fifty female parents participated in each phase. Each male fathered five children. You and I are part of the first phase. Unfortunately, the genetic modifications caused a defect that resulted in the miscarriage of eighty percent of the male embryos in that phase. Only five male children survived–those created from the cells of the

Greek father. That makes you and me, along with our other three half-brothers, part of an elite group, so to speak. I'm arranging a meeting for us soon. Please call me in the next couple of days. I hope you have a pleasant evening." The video screen darkened.

Maggie put her hand on Levin's shoulder. "This must be why Scott wanted to find you. I wonder why he knows so much about the Project already. He talks like he grew up around it."

"I don't know, but I'm tired of him leaving little bread crumbs for me to follow. Why doesn't he just call me?"

"Maybe he wants to rouse your curiosity first, to give you an invested interest. I think you should call him. Imagine, a few months ago, you didn't have any brothers, and now you have four. At least! You told me Rana has the same father. You must have more siblings."

He wished he shared her enthusiasm.

Chapter Seven

"Hello?"

"Scott. It's Levin." He sat in his car at the end of his work day, having decided that morning to make the call. He'd planned to ignore Scott's request for contact, but his curiosity about the other brothers had grown into an incessant distraction in the four days since watching the video.

"I'm glad you called. I've reached the other brothers more quickly than I anticipated. We're meeting in two weeks, in Denver."

Levin swallowed. *Two weeks?* "Well, that's convenient."

"Yeah, it works well for you. Daniel lives in Oklahoma City, but the others live on the coasts."

"All right. So where are we meeting?"

After Scott gave him the information, Levin ended the call and drove out of the parking lot.

****

Rana looked away from her laptop screen and out her bedroom window when a car pulled into the driveway. Levin left the car and approached the front door, and she walked downstairs to meet him. She hadn't spoken with him since the day they arrived home from San Diego.

"Hey, bro, I wondered when I'd see you around here again."

"Yeah." He rubbed his neck. "You want to go for a walk? I need to talk to you. Alone."

"Um, sure." She went into the house and fetched her sandals.

"I want to come, too," Dayla whined from the kitchen.

"Not this time." Rana left the house and walked with her brother. The air, crisp from an earlier rainstorm, gave her goosebumps.

"I, uh . . . I called Scott tonight."

Rana waited for him to elaborate, and when he didn't, she asked, "And?"

"On the night we came back into town, he emailed me a video." He told her about the defect in the first phase and about his four half-brothers. "So, when I spoke with him tonight, he said he's arranged a meeting for all of us in Denver in two weeks."

"That's convenient."

"That's what I said."

"You're going, right?"

He shrugged. "I haven't decided yet."

"You have to go. Maybe you'll get more answers about–you know, about our purpose."

"Our purpose?"

Rana wrung her hands. “Well, yeah. I mean, we wouldn’t exist if not for the Project. Our parents didn’t even live on the same continent. And not only that, they messed with our genes. They *modified* them. We’re GMOs!”

“I suppose. So?”

“So, no one really knows the long term effects of GMOs on our bodies. And our entire bodies are GMOs. What if we, I don’t know, randomly grow a third arm from the middle of our backs or something?”

He laughed.

She scowled. “I’m serious. You said so yourself– eighty percent of the boys in your phase died. That probably wouldn’t have happened if they hadn’t screwed with the DNA.” She couldn’t help but notice the irony of her position against GMOs in her debate: she had basically argued against the existence of herself and her siblings.

“Don’t worry about medical problems. I’m sure they would have discovered anything wrong with us by now–”

“Anyway, that’s not my point. Most people spend their young adult lives trying to figure out what to do with themselves–to find their purpose. But scientists designed us to fill someone else’s purpose. What does that mean for us and our lives? Can we do what we want, or do we have to do what the Project wants? Or what they designed us to do? They could be the same, but what if they’re not? Will they try to force us into doing something they want us to do? And what about Mom? Did she have us just for the money? Will she . . .” she paused to find her words, “turn us in to the Project so they can study us or something?”

Levin put a hand on her arm, stopping her from walking, and looked straight into her eyes. “Mom raised us. I don’t think she’s gonna hand us over to a research organization. And I don’t think the Project people will be that invasive, or we would have learned about them before now. But I’ll go to the meeting. Will that make you feel better?”

She nodded. “I want to go, too.”

“Not happening. Scott’s pursued me this whole time. I need to find out what he wants by myself.”

His response annoyed her, but she didn’t argue.

“And I promise to tell you if I start growing an arm from the middle of my back.” He smirked.

She punched him on the shoulder.

Chapter Eight

Levin pulled into a parking garage near the coffee shop where he and the other half-brothers had agreed to meet. He dreaded the gathering but didn't complain: he drove half an hour while the rest of the men traveled from all over the country. Scott had told him Denver was the most central place with a major airport, and it made sense to meet close to one of them. Levin got to be the lucky one. It also made it much harder for him to back out.

He arrived a little early, but he figured he'd order a coffee and wait for guys who looked like him to show up. How many heads would they turn in their gathering?

He didn't have to wait for an answer. Scott sat at a round table in the back corner of the dining area with two other men sporting black, wavy hair. One had tan skin and appeared shorter than the others. The other man had let his hair grow long enough for it to curl at the ends.

Levin approached the table as the three men stood to greet him. He shook hands with the long-haired one.

"Hi. I'm Levin."

"Daniel. Nice to meet you."

He shook Scott's hand, then the hand of the third man, who introduced himself as Jeremy.

As the men reclaimed their seats, Levin took the empty chair next to Daniel.

Levin couldn't help but compare his features to those of the other men at the table. Aside from the obvious difference in hair length, Daniel was a bit taller and thinner than Levin, and Jeremy looked like he spent quality time at the beach. Otherwise, he guessed strangers could easily identify them as brothers.

"Brent hasn't arrived yet," Scott said. "While we're waiting, how was everyone's trip into town?"

Jeremy and Daniel discussed their flights, and Levin joked about a cone zone he had to negotiate. As they spoke, Levin sensed movement in his peripheral vision and looked up. Another man strongly resembling those in the group stood by their table, though his slightly heavier build gave his face a rounder appearance, and his short haircut held no discernable wave.

"Hi. I'm Br…Brent Sutherland. S…s…sorry I'm late." He shook everyone's hand as they recited their names again. Brent sat next to Jeremy on the opposite side of the table from Levin, creating a gap between them. Scott sat in the middle of the semi-circle of brothers.

"Welcome. You're not late," Scott said. "Let's begin by telling a little bit about ourselves, if that's not too predictable. I thought you could each give us some information about your background, and then tell us what you thought of Project Renovatio when you first learned about it. Who would like to start?"

Levin scanned the other tables, the counter, his hands . . . anything to avoid having to speak first.

Finally, Daniel's voice permeated the silence. "I'll start." He sat up straighter. "Well, I'm Daniel Jackson. I live in Oklahoma City where I started medical school not too long ago. My sister, Janie, is twelve years old. She's a PR kid too, but we have different fathers." He sipped his large coffee. "When Scott told me my origins, and I followed up with my mom, I was excited. Oklahoma City holds the same appeal as dry toast. Honestly…" He grinned. "I thought this information might make it easier to meet girls. I mean, who doesn't want to hook up with a genetically gifted individual, am I right?"

The men laughed, though Levin doubted anyone else shared Daniel's sentiment. He came off as creepy.

Scott nodded. "Thank you, Daniel. Who would like to go next?"

"I will," replied a voice from across the table. "I'm Jeremy Ruiz. I live in Miami. I'm an assistant P.E. teacher at a middle school while I work on earning my own certification." Jeremy had a slight accent in his voice. "I have a sixteen year old brother named Eliot. When my mother told me about the Project, I was unsettled. I love my life. I have a great family, a wonderful job, and I'm engaged to my beautiful Renee."

A wide smile took over his face. He pulled his phone from his pocket and touched the screen a few times before turning it towards the group. The picture featured a stunning young lady with long black hair, tan skin, and dark eyes wearing a simple lavender sundress.

"I'm not anxious to change my life, but I am interested to see where this goes." He sat back and returned his phone to his pocket, indicating he'd finished his part of the sharing time.

Levin shifted in his seat. "I'll go next," He cleared his throat. "I'm Levin Davis. I live thirty minutes south of here. I'm a software developer. I have two sisters, Rana and Dayla. They're both children from the Project." He considered his next point, wondering how much he should share with the strangers. "My girlfriend's name is Maggie. She's in school earning her biology degree." He smiled against his will. "I don't have a picture in my phone to show you. She takes all the pictures of us."

Jeremy laughed.

"When I first heard about PR, I thought it was a bunch of bull meant to scam me somehow. I still don't understand parts of it, but maybe I'll get more answers today."

"Thank you, Levin. I think you will. Brent, would you mind telling us about yourself?" Scott held his smile for the duration of the introductions.

He shook his head. "I'm Br…Br…Brent Sutherland. I'm an a…a…auto mechanic from sss…Seattle." He stopped talking and scanned the group.

"Brent, feel free to continue as you're comfortable," Scott said, as if the two had discussed this possibility prior to the meeting.

"Th…thanks. I've al…always stammered…b…b…but it gets worse…w…w…when I'm nervous." He chuckled anxiously.

Levin leaned towards Brent after an uncomfortable pause. "My buddy at work has a stammer. If he has a hard time, I ask him questions and he answers them. Seems to help." Levin offered the suggestion cautiously. He could only guess how Brent would receive it.

Brent nodded.

"All right. Do you have any siblings?"

"Y…yes. My b…brother, Isaiah. He's sixteen."

"Okay. And what did you think when Scott told you about the Project?"

"I was s…s…scared I would h…have to talk to people."

The men laughed. Brent grinned and sat back in his seat.

Scott smiled. "Thank you, Brent. Now, I'd like to share more about myself. Jeremy asked me earlier if I grew up around the Project or if I work there. The answer is, both. My mother is married to Steven Craig, the geneticist who took the lead for the San Diego division of Project Renovatio." He kept his arms on the table and grasped his coffee cup with both hands. "He had her screened as part of the training for his techs and discovered she qualified to participate."

"Wasn't that awkward?" Daniel asked.

"I guess not. He gave her the option to take part in the Project the same way he offered it to your mothers. They discussed having children before, and my dad–Dr. Craig–chose to raise me as his own son. They gave me my mother's maiden name to reduce any suspicion of favoritism on his part." He sipped his coffee. "I have no siblings. My mother carried a girl child four years after I was born, but the baby didn't survive because of a medical problem my mom had. They opted not to try again. Unlike the rest of you, I grew up knowing the nature of my existence. In fact, you'll have to forgive me if I seem unconcerned with how learning about PR has affected you. It has simply been a fact of my life. I work for the organization now, kind of as an outreach guy."

"Is that what they wrote on your business card?" Levin asked. The men laughed.

Scott finished chuckling. "No. I don't need business cards. I bring PR children the knowledge of their existence as it becomes appropriate and necessary. Which takes me to my next point." He turned his attention to Jeremy. "You recently became engaged, to Renee."

"Yes. So?"

"So, your situation has prompted this meeting for all of you. Before I begin explaining, though, I want to tell you first as an employee of Project Renovatio and then as your brother."

The conversation had taken a strange turn, and Levin wished he hadn't mentioned Maggie in the introductions. Scott's smile gave way to a serious tone.

"When Project Renovatio started, they tried to plan ahead, genetically speaking. They planned to create 150 males and 150 females who would grow up and pass their genetic information to their children. From a sociological standpoint, they didn't worry about PR kids pairing with those who might . . . diminish the genetic advantages given to them. People tend to choose partners who are like themselves. Smart people choose smart partners; athletes tend to choose other fit individuals, and so on. Now, we five are the only male survivors of the first phase. Because of that, PR can't risk losing our genetic advantages in the general population."

"W…what does that m….mean?" Brent asked.

"It means they want us to find partners from among the other PR kids–obviously from the ones with different fathers. If our partners share our traits, we will likely pass them on to our children."

Jeremy shifted in his seat and leaned forward. "It's nice they want that, but what gives them the right to suggest it?"

"They don't have the right, per se. But we exist because of PR, and therefore, they feel they have a claim to us. They want to establish an ever-increasing group of advantaged humans well before it's needed. The Project took a big blow when they lost most of the males in the first phase. This plan will allow them to recover."

Levin clenched his fist under the table. "Help *them* recover? You're talking about our lives. They can't make us do anything." He tried to swallow the foul taste at the back of his throat. "We didn't know they existed two months ago. And why wait until Jeremy gets engaged to tell us this? They must know we won't go for it." He spoke more for himself than for Jeremy.

"You're right. And now I'd like to start explaining as your brother." He scanned the place, leaned in towards the group, and lowered his voice. "Personally, I think the whole suggestion sucks. Our mothers–well, your mothers–signed a contract saying they would carry and raise you and report your progress back to the Project. That's it. There's nothing about monitoring you past the age of eighteen, and there is no mention of whom we should choose as partners. So," he glanced at the ceiling and sighed, "you should all tell your mothers to stop communicating with Project Renovatio. They still track your younger siblings. As long as PR monitors them, it monitors you. You can't assume they'll stop caring about you just because you're over eighteen."

"That means our mothers would have to give up the money," Daniel said.

"Yes, it does. But you, and she, need to ask yourselves if allowing a research organization to monitor and possibly control you is worth the money."

Levin rubbed his neck. "Why tell us this? If you work for the Project, you risk losing your job."

"I'm aware of the risk. When PR told me to find you and tell you what they want, it made me sick to my stomach. Jeremy, you obviously love your fiancée very much. Levin, you seem to have strong feelings for your girlfriend as well. I can honestly say I understand how you feel. When the Project brought me this assignment, I had been dating Jocelyn for nearly a year. She was lovely, intelligent…" he pursed his lips and looked at the ceiling again, as if fighting back tears, "and I wanted to marry her. But my dad–Dr. Craig–insisted I break it off with her and seek a partner from the girls in PR. He implied her safety would be at risk if I didn't. So," he exhaled slowly, "I did. I told her I didn't want a serious relationship after all. I believe I protected her." With a shaking hand, he brought his coffee to his lips.

"What do you mean her safety would be at risk?" Jeremy leaned forward and squinted.

Scott set down his cup. "I don't know, exactly. Like I said, he implied it. His exact words were, 'It would be better *for her* if you weren't with her.' Because of my position in the Project, I couldn't do anything about it. But I realized I could help the four of you avoid the same fate. Tell your mothers to break communications with PR, and I highly recommend moving your family at least to a new city, if not a new state. And stay vigilant. They won't go quietly. They have many people stationed around PR families. If you feel watched, it's because someone's watching you."

"This is crazy." Jeremy rose from his chair and paced near the table. He rubbed his forehead and closed his eyes. "What if we do notice something, like evidence PR tracks us? Do we just keep moving? Stay one step ahead?"

"That's what I would do. But if you break off your relationships, they will leave you alone."

Levin dug his nails into his leg. He couldn't stomach the possibility of breaking up with Maggie, but she might not want to carry the risk.

What if she didn't?

Daniel broke the following silence. "Okay, so let's pretend we all go for this and try to find girls from the PR population. How do we do that? The only ones we know are our sisters."

"That's the next part of my job. I'm supposed to organize a gathering where all the PR kids will meet. It won't happen soon, though. I have to wait until the kids in the final phase–the current ten-year-olds–are old enough to learn about PR. We think that will be when they're fourteen or so. By then, all kids in the first four phases will be over eighteen. The timing is tricky because those in the last two phases will be too young for anyone, but at least you will all know about each other. For now, I'm supposed to tell you to stop dating just anybody and wait for the gathering."

"What do they expect from us? To pair and breed? What about the rest of our lives? Our careers? Don't we get the opportunity to date, like everyone else?" Daniel asked.

"Of course you can have your lives, but PR plans to study the genetic makeup of our children. So in a way, yes, they want us to breed, as you say. The Project wants you not to date so you'll be available when you meet the PR girls," Scott said.

"They want us to wait for them? They can't be serious." Levin scripted in his head what to say to his mother.

"I'm afraid they are. Look, I realize they're trying to bully you. But it's *you* they're afraid of. Don't forget, the government supports PR, and they want to keep the whole thing quiet because those outside the Project wouldn't look kindly on a group 'playing God' by creating its own people, so to speak. PR has funding to protect, and if they lose the support of certain department heads, it's over. You have the power to bring them down, and they know it. They also know if the public learns about PR, you–we–will likely be alienated as well, as those who were 'never meant to be.' We all have something to lose. If not for the disastrous loss of males in the first phase, you probably still wouldn't know the truth of your existence. It's safer for them if we remain comfortably anonymous.

But since that can't happen, they will try to exert their influence over you."

Silence covered the group.

Jeremy stood near the table with his arms crossed. "Okay. I need to leave. It was nice meeting you all. I'm going to try to catch the next flight home." He left the group and walked out the door.

"I guess we're done," Daniel said.

"Apparently. I hope you all consider what I've told you." Scott pulled three cards from his wallet and distributed them to the remaining men. "This number goes to a disposable cell phone PR doesn't know I have. Use it if PR gives you trouble, and I'll do my best to help you." He stood. "Remember, from now on, you have two choices: stay on their good side, or disappear."

Chapter Nine

Rana started her third shift at Safeway in the produce section. Her boss had hired her to restock general merchandise, but he allowed her to branch out when he saw how quickly she completed her tasks without getting tired. She suspected her efficiency came from the fact that the job offered an effective distraction from what she learned about PR, and with Levin meeting their brothers today, she expected to double her productivity.

As she held bags of carrots, waiting for the sprinklers to finish so her arms wouldn't get wet, a tap on the shoulder startled her. She turned to see an unexpected face.

Jason.

"Oh my gosh. You scared me." She stared at the carrots, willing her heart rate to slow.

He laughed. "Sorry. Hey, I was wondering if you planned to use that number I gave you."

“Yeah. Sorry. I’ve been busy since I got back from my trip, and since I got this job.” She gestured to her surroundings, as if they offered a reasonable explanation. In reality, she hadn’t called because she couldn’t decide exactly what to say. “I want to earn enough money to buy a car before school starts.”

“That’s all right. Listen, my parents and little sister are leaving town this weekend, and my mom said I can invite a few friends over on Saturday. You wanna come?” He held his charming grin through every word.

“Uh . . . yeah. I don’t think I’m working that day. Only, can I bring my friend, Jacey?”

“Jacey Brewer? Sure, I guess. She’s nice.” His shoulders slumped a little. “Anyway, come by any time after seven.” He squeezed her shoulder and walked away.

Her heart melted right there in the produce section.

****

Rana changed clothes at least ten times, removing each item in disgust as it didn’t meet her qualifications for inclusion in the perfect outfit. The evidence of her clothing failures cluttered her bedroom floor. She doubted Jacey put this much thought into her outfit, and she felt a little guilty for stringing her friend along to a gathering where Rana planned to flirt with a boy at every opportunity.

She decided on khaki shorts and a purple top with a leafy pattern at the same time Jacey rang the doorbell. They walked the four blocks to Jason’s house side by side.

“So, whose house are we going to?” Jacey asked.

“Jason Burke. We’re in debate together.” Rana looked straight ahead, hoping Jacey wouldn’t notice her apprehension.

“And why did he invite you?”

“I guess he saw me at the store and recognized me.”

“Huh. Okay.” Jacey kept her eyes on Rana as they walked.

Rana felt Jacey staring at her. “Fine. He gave me his number before school was out, but I didn’t call him because I’ve had a huge crush on him since Christmas and I have problems, you know, forming words when he’s around. There.” She huffed.

“Now was that so hard?” Jacey smiled. “I knew you liked him, by the way.”

“What? How?”

“You don’t exactly hide your feelings well, Rana Davis.” Jacey put her arm around Rana’s shoulders and gave her a squeeze.

They arrived at Jason’s house a few minutes later. Some random teenagers had gathered on the front porch, and they stopped talking to each other and glared at the girls as they climbed the stairs to the door. Rana recognized one of the girls from her English class.

They entered the house. Jason stood in the kitchen, talking to another guy and holding a plastic cup. Pizza boxes, clean plastic plates, plates containing partially eaten pizza, and beer and soda bottles cluttered the island, and the means for making mixed drinks–cranberry juice, orange juice, and vodka–rested on the counter at the far end of the room. Rana had heard about crowded parties powered by alcohol, but she hadn't been to one before tonight.

Jacey walked into the kitchen, but Rana stayed in the doorway. Jason smiled at her, said a couple words to the other guy, and approached her.

"Hi, Rana, I'm glad you're here."

Her heart fluttered when he said her name.

"Can I make you a drink?" He lifted his cup and shook it slightly, placed his hand on the doorframe near her head, and leaned towards her with his whole body. Her heart raced at his closeness.

"Um . . . no, thanks. Maybe later." She grinned at him, compelled to say something else but unable to decide what. Why wouldn't her brain cooperate? "I'll just get some pizza for now." She resisted the urge to smack herself on the forehead. Talking to him came much more easily when it involved a structured debate.

"Okay, sure." He stepped away from her and gestured with his cup towards the counter without removing his hand from the doorframe. "Help yourself."

"Thanks." She walked by him and towards Jacey.

"Wow. Smooth," Jacey whispered as she selected a large slice of cheese pizza.

"Shut up. Like you know how to flirt."

Rana put a slice of pepperoni pizza on her plate despite her nerves crowding her appetite. She nibbled on it occasionally while she and Jacey wandered through different rooms, eventually landing in a family room where many of the other teenagers had gathered. They passed the already overcrowded couch and settled on the floor against a wall, facing each other.

“So, this is fun.” Sarcasm dripped from Jacey’s words.

“Sorry. We’ll finish our food, say ‘hi’ to a few people, and then we’ll go. Okay?”

Jacey nodded as she took a bite of her pizza. Rana scanned the crowd. Many of the teens laughed and talked much more loudly than necessary. A couple made out in the corner like they had the place to themselves.

Rana shook her head. Why had Jason approached her? She preferred watching movies with Jacey to participating in something like this.

The girls finished their food and made their way to the kitchen. Jason met them and addressed Jacey.

“Hey, you mind if I steal your friend for a little bit?” He winked at Rana.

“Okay, but have her back by midnight.” Jacey strolled across the kitchen, stationed herself by a bowl of chips, and talked with a nerdy looking guy who appeared to have taken residence there.

Jason set his drink on the counter, grasped Rana’s wrist, and pulled her into a hallway. He stopped in the middle of the hall, positioned her back against the wall, and placed his hand near her head, the same way he had done when she stood in the doorway. Was he holding himself up? The smell of alcohol wafted from his breath.

“So, Rana,” he said as he used his fingers to twirl her curly hair, “I’ve noticed you seem . . . interested in me.”

Heat rushed to her face. “Yeah…”

“Is it true?” He stared into her eyes.

Adrenaline surged through her. “I guess. I mean, I think you’re cute–”

He pressed his lips into hers. She tried to match the motions of his lips and tongue, but his breath distracted her from what should have been a momentous occasion. Her shirt moved as his hand traveled up her stomach and stopped on her breast.

Her eyes shot open, and she put her hands on his shoulders, shoving him away with all of her strength.

A moment later, Jason removed himself from the deep impression in the wall his body created.

Mortified, Rana’s hands flew to her mouth. “I’m sorry…surprised me…I’m not ready…oh my gosh…” She finally gave up, ran to the kitchen, grabbed Jacey’s wrist, and pulled her out the front door.

Chapter Ten

Levin spent the rest of the afternoon visiting with Daniel and Brent. He and Brent easily connected, but Daniel filled the time with awkward jokes and obnoxious laughter. They ended their meeting by exchanging phone numbers and email addresses. Unlike Jeremy, Daniel and Brent had both planned short trips in Denver. Levin told them he would try to meet with them again after work one day before they left, but he only half meant it. He needed to get to Maggie.

Thirty minutes later, he knocked on the door of her apartment.

"Hey." Her smile quickly dissipated. "What's going on?"

"Can I come in?"

"Oh, yeah." Maggie stepped back. The smell of cleanser filled the space, and she wore old workout pants, a grubby Pearl Jam T-shirt, and a ponytail. A plugged-in vacuum sat in the kitchen. He made his way to the couch, trying to squelch his envy of her uneventful day. She seated herself next to him.

"Well," he cleared his throat, "I met my brothers."

"Isn't that a good thing?"

"Yes and no." He told her the basic information about each brother, including their names, where they lived, and their jobs. He added irrelevant details to delay arriving at the subject he dreaded.

"They sound like nice guys," she said.

"They are, but there's more."

He described Scott's situation and warning, watching her face reflect increasing concern as he talked. His heart ached when he finally reached the ultimatum.

"So, basically, PR wants me to marry a PR girl, or we could be in some kind of danger."

She sat with her mouth agape for a few seconds. "What does that mean?"

"I don't know, and I don't think Scott does either. He said Dr. Craig implied the threat." Levin stared at his shoes as he considered how to say the next point, his stomach twisting into a knot. He sighed and looked Maggie in the eyes. "They threatened Scott's girlfriend, not Scott. He said you're the one in danger if we stay together. I want you to know I understand…" He closed his eyes and inhaled. "I understand if you don't want to stay with me. I'm not expecting you to place yourself in danger for me."

He opened his eyes. Maggie wiped a tear from her cheek with her wrist.

"This is crap." She rose from the couch and stood across from him, keeping one hand on her hip and using the other to animate her speech. "Does Scott work for PR or not? What does he have to gain from telling you this? He could lose his job, at best, or be in 'some kind of danger' himself, at worst."

Levin kept his calm tone. "I don't understand that either. I figure he feels loyalty to us as a brother."

"Oh, well that makes it okay then!" She took a long, shaking breath. "Do you think we're in danger?"

He shrugged. "I haven't seen anything directly suggesting it. I realized something on the way here, though."

"What?"

"We have a third choice. Scott said we do what PR wants or disappear." He paused as he gathered his words. "The third choice is we fight. If we show them they don't own us, and we challenge their authority–if you can call it that–over us, maybe they'll leave us alone."

"Fight? Aren't you the guy who told me he doesn't like confrontation? And how can we fight? We don't know anything about them."

"You're right. We'd have to wait for them to make a move to see what we're dealing with. And as for the confrontation…" He stood and put his fingers on her cheek. "I guess I never had a good reason to be confrontational before."

His love for her washed over him as he caressed her soft skin and gazed into her eyes, and his whole being silently begged her to say she would stick with him in spite of the threat. His throat tightened at the thought of having to leave her.

Maggie's expression softened. She took his hand and held it in both of hers. "I'm staying with you. I'm not scared." She stretched up and kissed him, putting her hand on the back of his neck. The softness of her lips sent chills through his body. When she released, she kept her eyes closed and her face an inch from his. "I love you." She opened her eyes.

Levin framed her face with his hands and returned her kiss, vowing to do whatever he had to do to keep this captivating woman in his life.

****

The next morning, Levin drove to his mother's house. Rana likely wanted to hear how the meeting went. He wished he wanted to tell her.

He knocked twice to announce his presence, let himself in through the unlocked door, and walked to the kitchen. Walt slept in a recliner in the family room. Footsteps sounded on the stairs behind him and he turned.

Rana stood before him; tear-streaked makeup covered her face, she wore wrinkled clothes, and her frizzy hair obscured her usually tight curls.

"What happened to you?" Levin asked a little more loudly than he intended. Rana tipped her head towards Walt and motioned for Levin to follow her through the kitchen to the back porch. Once outside, she closed the thick, glass door, and they sat in lawn chairs overlooking the weedy yard.

Levin glared at her, waiting for an explanation.

Rana stared at her feet. "I went to a party last night." She sniffed. "At Jason's house."

"Oh?" His brotherly instincts engaged, and he leaned towards her a bit. "Who's Jason?"

"A boy from school. It was awful. Dozens of people I don't know or don't like showed up. There was alcohol. Jason tried . . . to take advantage of me."

Levin put his elbows on his knees. “What do you mean, ‘tried’?”

She wiped her tears with her open hands. “He pulled me into a hallway. He couldn’t have done anything more than he did. He kissed me and . . . stuck his hand up my shirt.” She took a shaking breath. “I freaked…” She hiccupped. “Freaked out, and I threw him into the wall.”

He laughed. “Good for you.” He leaned back in his chair, relieved.

She scowled. “How can you say that? I made a big dent in the wall with his body.”

“Impressive.”

“Will you please stop?” She glared at him. “I’m only a little upset about what Jason did. We’d been flirting, and I let him kiss me. I just didn’t expect him to do *that* in front of all those people.” She focused on the ground, her embarrassment draping her like a blanket. “I’m more upset that I threw him into the wall. What if his parents come after me?”

“Seriously?”

She squinted at him.

“You really are a good girl. Here’s the deal: he probably didn’t have permission to host that kind of party, he certainly shouldn’t have been drinking, and he got fresh with you. You had every right to throw him into the wall. If he’s smart, he’ll make up some story about how he tripped into it. Oh, and he’d better stay away from you after this, or I’ll have to get all ‘big brothery’ on him.” He winked.

“You’re right.” She wiped her tears again. “So, how did the meeting go?”

Levin sighed, and for the second time replayed yesterday's events, including Scott's warning.

"They can't tell you who to marry. Who do they think they are? Did you tell Maggie yet?"

"Yeah. I let her decide if she wanted to take the risk of being with me." He paused as a wide smile occupied his face. "She said she'll stay with me."

Rana watched him for a moment. "And I take it you're not breaking up with her."

Levin chuckled. "No."

She stood. "That means we should meet her. Mom's getting Dayla from camp right now. We can invite Maggie over tonight. Let's have some fun instead of worrying about PR."

"Whoa, hold on. We need to plan this in advance."

"Why? Does she work on Sundays?"

"No, but–"

"Then call her, you big dork. I'll call Mom and tell her what's going on."

Rana went into the house, leaving Levin alone on the porch. With nothing else to do, he found Maggie's contact in his phone.

Five minutes later, Rana poked her head out the door. "Mom says she can't wait to meet Maggie. She's stopping at the grocery store on her way home." She had returned to her old, pre-party self.

"Okay. I told Maggie I'll pick her up at six."

"Good. I'm going to take a shower." She left him alone without further ceremony. He walked around the house to return to his car.

Chapter Eleven

Rana turned off the shower, wrapped herself in a towel, and headed to her room. Her rejected outfits from the previous night still covered the floor. She picked up a pair of denim shorts and a green top to wear for the day, got dressed, and began putting the rest of her clothes away as she tried to bury her memories of the party. Her talk with Levin had helped, but the sick feeling that insisted on occupying her stomach didn't get the message.

In the middle of hanging a skirt, the front door slammed and footsteps raced up the stairs. Dayla came bounding in and plopped herself on Rana's bed.

"Hey girlie. How was camp?"

"Awesome. I got to do my own experiment on anything I wanted. I did mine on roly poly bugs. I got to go swimming too. Do you know how pool water kills germs? My friend, Alicia, did that for her experiment. We shared a cabin. She's really nice and *super* smart. Mom says I can call her to come visit. She only lives an hour from here."

"Neat. I'm glad you made a friend. Did Mom tell you what we're doing tonight?"

Dayla giggled. "Yeah. We're meeting Levin's *girl*-friend." She put her hand over her mouth, fell back onto the bed, and laughed almost uncontrollably.

"All right, giggle bug. You probably need to take a shower. I'll help Mom with the groceries."

"Okay." Dayla rose from the bed and skipped to the bathroom. Rana made her way downstairs.

"Good morning, sweetie. Do you know if Maggie likes chicken?" Liz held a package of drumsticks.

"I'm sure she does. Who doesn't?"

"But what if she's a vegetarian? I'd better call Levin." She retrieved her phone from her purse.

"What's going on?" a gruff voice asked from behind Rana. Walt cleared his throat.

Rana twisted around to face him. "Oh. We're having Levin and his girlfriend over for dinner. We haven't met her before."

"Really?"

"Yeah." She wasn't sure how to talk to Walt. They got along fairly well before his deployment, but conversations with him became more difficult after he returned.

"What's her name?"

"Maggie. Do . . . you want to join us?" She'd assumed he'd stay upstairs by himself for the evening.

"I think I might." He nodded as he climbed the stairs. A minute later, Dayla shrieked from the kids' bathroom, likely from the sudden change in water temperature caused by Walt turning on the shower in the master bathroom. Rana laughed.

"Levin said she eats chicken. Whew." Her mom smiled and gave her a hug.

"Wow. You're pretty excited."

"Of course I am. She's the first *real* significant other to come into our house. And Levin's getting old enough to think about settling down."

"He's only twenty, Mom."

"Almost twenty-one." She resumed emptying the grocery bags. "What did Walt want?"

"I think he wants to attend the party. Kinda strange."

"Not really. His counselor wants him to start socializing more. Maybe I'll give him a haircut."

"Good idea."

****

By that evening, everyone in the family wore presentable clothes. Even Walt cared about his appearance. He looked sharp with his new haircut, clean shave, and bright outfit.

Dayla waited impatiently by the window. Finally, she squealed, "They're here. Wait–there's someone else with them."

"Huh?" Rana walked to the window to assess the situation. Levin walked hand-in-hand with a young woman, and another guy wearing a Broncos T-shirt and denim shorts followed close behind.

Levin knocked and waited on the porch, a formality he would normally skip. Dayla rushed to answer the door, smiling so widely her cheeks must have hurt.

"Hey, Dayla. Did you have fun at camp?" Levin asked before entering the house.

"Yeah. Is this Maggie?"

He laughed. "Yes. Maggie, meet my little sister–"

Dayla rushed through the door and wrapped her arms around Maggie, who laughed.

After hugging Levin, Dayla grabbed his hand and pulled him inside, dragging the smiling trio indoors and stopping in front of Rana.

Levin gestured to Rana but kept his eyes on Maggie. "This is my other sister, Rana." The girls shook hands and exchanged 'nice to meet you's.

Rana was struck by Maggie's appearance: she wore green khaki capris and a simple white blouse, and her smooth, brown hair draped over her shoulders. Rana couldn't help herself. She looked at her brother and said simply, "Nice job."

Maggie brought her hand to her mouth and laughed.

Levin blushed. "Yeah. Thanks." He gestured to the man standing on his other side. "This is Brent, one of my brothers from the meeting with Scott. I hope you don't mind me inviting him; I thought you might like to meet one of your brothers."

"Oh, um, of course. Hi, Brent. It's nice to meet you." She shook his hand.

"Nice to m…m…meet you, too."

Rana nervously eyed the group and pointed to the kitchen. "Mom and Walt are on the back porch. Walt's working the barbecue grill, if you can believe that."

Levin's eyes widened. "I'm not sure I can."

"Can I get anyone a drink?" Rana asked as they walked towards the kitchen. The three guests told Rana what they wanted and walked outside while Rana and Dayla stayed behind to fix the drinks.

"What did Levin mean, 'meet your brother'? Is he my brother too?" Dayla asked.

Oh, right. They'd kept most of the Project Renovatio information from Dayla before now. "Not exactly. I'll tell you about it later, okay? It's a long story."

"Okay." Dayla seemed satisfied. "I'm going to give Maggie her tea. Isn't she pretty?" The girl wouldn't stop smiling.

"Yes. She's lovely." Rana gave her sister a slight shove on the back and followed holding the other drinks.

The girls joined the group on the porch. Liz, Maggie, and Levin sat in a small circle of chairs, Brent stood behind them with his hands in the pockets of his shorts, and Walt manned the grill. Rana walked to the side of the house and fetched extra chairs.

"Maggie, we are so excited to meet you. Please, tell us about yourself. We're very interested to learn what caught Levin's eye." Liz glanced in Levin's direction.

"Thanks, Mom." Levin shifted in his seat.

Rana gave Brent a chair, unfolded one for herself, and sat outside the circle.

Maggie took Levin's hand. She sat at the front edge of her chair, as if she didn't think they'd allow her to take up the whole thing. "It's fine. Well, I'm a student. I'm working on my biology degree. I work at the campus library to make some extra money. I have an eighteen-year-old brother named Grayson. Um…"

She glanced at Levin. “I guess that’s it.” She laughed nervously.

“Biology. Strong choice. What do you plan to do with that?” Liz asked.

“Ultimately, I hope to go to medical school and become a forensic pathologist.”

“Wow. Impressive.”

“Thank you. I’ve learned quite a bit. I’m anxious to take the next step.”

“Wonderful.” Liz smiled at Maggie for a moment before turning her attention to Brent. “And I’m pleasantly surprised to meet you, Brent, as we all are, I’m sure. Are you a friend of Levin’s?”

Rana froze. Her mother didn’t know about Levin’s meeting with his brothers. Rana braced herself for Brent’s response. Thankfully, Levin answered before Brent could.

“He’s my brother, Mom.”

“What?” Liz looked at Levin and Brent in quick succession before turning her attention to Dayla. “Go inside for a little while. We need to have an adult conversation. I’ll come get you when we’re done, okay?”

Dayla scowled and slumped her shoulders before entering the house.

“I’m ssss….sorry to s…s…surprise you like that, ma’am.”

“No, please. Don’t be sorry. Levin, would you mind filling me in?”

“Sure. I met with Scott yesterday. Well, with Scott and with our other half-brothers. Brent is one of them. He’s from Seattle.”

She looked at Brent, who nodded.

"Only five male embryos survived in the first phase of the Project. Scott, Brent, Daniel, Jeremy, and me. The rest were miscarried because something went wrong when they monkeyed with the DNA. We all have the same Greek father, so they're Rana's brothers too." Levin went on to describe Scott's involvement in the Project, what happened with Scott's girlfriend, and what Scott told them about marrying a PR girl.

"That's terrible. They can't tell you how to live." His mother stared outside the group and took a sip from her glass.

"He didn't think so either, but he couldn't do anything about it, as close as he is to the Project. He did suggest another option, though."

"What option?"

"He said we should either do what the Project wants–meaning I marry a PR girl–or we sever communication with them and try to disappear."

Liz faced Maggie. "Scott said they threatened his girlfriend. It's possible you're the one in danger here. What do you want to do?"

Maggie leaned back. "Frankly, I want to stay with Levin. I'm not going to let whatever this is dictate how I live. It could turn out to be nothing at all."

"Mom," Levin said, "you have to stop communicating with the Project. And we need to move, at least to another city. That's just a start."

"Levin, it's not that simple. I signed an agreement. If I stop communicating, I lose the money. And I seriously doubt they will leave me alone."

He leaned forward in his chair. "That's why we should prepare to stand our ground. Even if we move, they can easily find us. But we can't let this organization, or whatever it is, control our lives. They have no right to make me do what they want."

Walt surprised Rana by adding to the argument from the grill. "Liz, you know I can protect you. We have enough money between my disability and your job. You should do what Levin is asking."

Liz glared at Walt, apparently speechless, so Rana took the opportunity to interject. "Mom, do you think the Project owns us?"

"No, of course not. That's ridiculous."

"Then the choice is easy. Levin should be able to choose a partner. I should be able to do what I want for a career. If they think they can control Levin like this, why would they stop there? No. You have to stop communicating with them."

Her mother sat in silence for a moment. "You're right. What do I do? Write a letter?"

Silence covered the group until Levin offered a solution. "Yeah, I guess. Like a resignation letter. Say you're surrendering the money in exchange for our privacy. We'll hope that's enough."

Chapter Twelve

The rest of the evening went smoothly. Rana and her family enjoyed Maggie's company, and Brent grew so comfortable his stammer occurred less frequently, though he talked noticeably less than anyone else, including Walt. Rana made sure to exchange email addresses with Brent before he left.

The next day, Liz wrote and sent both electronic and paper copies of her resignation letter to Project Renovatio. During the following weeks, everyone stayed highly guarded: they closely watched their surroundings for strange people, made sure to keep the doors locked, and Liz took time off work to monitor her daughters. When nothing suspicious occurred, life returned to what they called normal, aside from Walt being more engaged with the family than Rana had seen before.

Rana worked many hours of overtime at the grocery store and figured she'd have enough money to buy a respectable car a few weeks before school started. She even received a promotion, which didn't include much in the way of changing responsibilities, but she did get a raise. Her job would have been perfect except for one detail: Jason knew he could find her there. She still felt angry and embarrassed about what happened at the party, and she wasn't interested in discussing it with him. On a late night shift, though, as she unloaded a box of canned tomatoes, she looked up and momentarily connected with a pair of familiar eyes.

Jason approached her. "Hi, Rana. I hoped you'd be working tonight."

Her mind filled with an emotion she couldn't name, but it felt like a cross between frustration and relief. "Oh, okay. Yep, here I am." She put two cans on the shelf. "Can I help you find something? We close in twenty minutes."

He laughed. Apparently, he took her question as a joke. "No. I just wanted to make sure you're okay. I haven't been able to find you since the party."

"I've worked in the back a lot the past couple weeks." *By design*, she thought.

"Anyway, I want to tell you I'm really sorry."

"What for?" She avoided eye contact and continued loading the shelf.

He put his hands in his pockets and stared at the floor. "Well, for how I acted. My parents thought I invited a few friends. It kinda got out of hand–friends inviting more friends, that kind of thing. Some kids I barely know brought the drinks. If it makes you feel any better, I got into huge trouble."

She laughed. "Yeah, that helps a little." She intentionally met his eyes for the first time, weighing her next question. "What did you tell them about the wall?"

He shifted his feet and brought his hand to the back of his neck. "I told them I wrestled with one of my friends and I fell into it. They made me fix it."

Rana smiled. "Good."

"You're really strong." He rubbed his shoulder. "Have you ever considered boxing?" He grinned.

"Um, no. Thanks for the suggestion, though." She gestured with the cans she held. "I need to finish stocking these shelves."

He nodded. "Yeah, okay. Anyway, I just wanted you to know I feel terrible. It's bothered me since it happened, and I wish I could take it back. I hope we can still hang out, if you want."

She pursed her lips. "I dunno. I'll talk to you later, okay?"

He nodded, looked away, and left the way he entered without buying anything. He'd visited only to talk to her. Maybe he meant what he said.

****

Levin remained highly guarded after his mother sent the letters to Project Renovatio, even after weeks passed and nothing came from them. He glanced over his shoulder more often at work, and he called Maggie so frequently to check on her that she told him to stop so she wouldn't get in trouble at her job. When he wasn't completely paranoid about the Project, however, he enjoyed settling into a normal existence.

He and Maggie continued dating as though the meeting with Scott hadn't taken place. The weekend after he brought her to his mother's house, she invited him to meet her parents and brother, and they all seemed to approve of him as a partner for Maggie.

Tonight, as they watched a movie together, he held her in his arms, breathed in the clean scent of her hair, and imagined having the freedom to hold her close whenever he wanted. Since the day she said she'd stay with him in the face of a threat, he'd dreamed of spending every evening with her, waking next to her every morning, and of building a life with her.

She squeezed his arms closer to her body, and in that moment, he couldn't imagine wanting to be anywhere else. As he leaned over to kiss her, his phone rang from the kitchen.

****

Rana peered through the passenger window and the darkness surrounding her mother's house, then to her coworker sitting next to her. "Thanks for the ride home. I'll return the favor when I get a car."

Katelyn laughed. "The way you're going, that'll happen next week. Hey, who was that guy who came in tonight?"

"Oh. He knows me from school. I'll fill you in later." She left the car and waved to Katelyn.

Rana walked up the path to the front door as Katelyn drove away. Fishing her keys from her purse, Rana squinted at the doorknob. Why hadn't her mother turned on the porch light? She turned to the front window; the interior was equally dark.

Liz had told her she'd wait up, but maybe she got too tired.

Rana put her key to the lock and froze when the door pushed into the house. Someone had left it open.

Her pulse quickened, and she reached for her phone in her pocket. As she debated who to call, she leaned towards the door and listened.

Silence.

Reaching her hand into the narrow space between the open door and the frame, Rana flipped both switches inside, turning on the porch light and the lamp in the front room. She poked her head inside, then pulled back to the porch a second later.

Whoever left the door cracked could still be here.

But it could be nothing–maybe Walt didn't close it all the way after checking the mail.

Rana took a long breath and gently pushed the door open.

Not seeing anyone, she slowly entered the house. A spray of red on the wall in the front room drew her attention, which moved to the red spots on the carpet.

Her throat tightened, and she grabbed her phone. At the same moment she opened her recent contacts, something down the hall, lying in the kitchen doorway, stopped her.

A body. Walt's body.

She dropped her phone on the tile, rushed to him, and shook his shoulder. "Walt." He didn't respond, so she put both hands on his arm and shook harder. "Walt, wake up."

No response.

She put her fingers on his neck. The beat of his pulse pushed back, but his breathing sounded shallow. There was no blood on or around him, and he didn't appear wounded. The blood in the front room must have come from someone else.

Oh, God.

“Mom?” she called into the silent house.

She hurried back to her phone. The screen cracked in the fall, but it still functioned. As she ran from room to room in search of her mother, she tapped the first name in her recent contact list. Her heart pounded in her ears.

****

Maggie sat up. “It’s late. Who could that be?”

Levin stood, retrieved his phone, and checked the ID. “Rana? It’s really late for her to call.” He answered. “Hey.”

“You have to come home. Quick! Something happened to Mom.”

“Wait, what? What happened?” Levin turned away from Maggie and leaned against the counter, focusing on Rana’s words.

“In the living room . . . blood on the wall . . . Mom’s gone . . . Walt won’t wake up . . .”

He paced. “Okay, Rana, stop. I need you to listen. You need to hang up now and call the police. But first, do you know where Dayla is?”

“She went to her friend’s house. Alicia.”

“Okay, I’m on my way. Call 9-1-1.” He disconnected and held his phone in his shaking hand.

Maggie put her hand on his shoulder. “I’ll drive. You can tell me what she said on the way.”

Levin wrung his hands and bounced his leg during the twenty-minute ride. What would they find there? What had Rana seen?

Police cars crowded the street in front of his mother’s house. An ambulance sat double-parked, and paramedics loaded Walt into it.

Levin ran to them before they left. “Excuse me, can you tell me what happened to him?”

The young man assessed Levin before responding. “Who are you?”

“Levin. Walt’s my stepdad. What’s wrong with him?”

“We don’t know yet. It looks like someone drugged him. He has weak vital signs, but he should recover. We’re taking him to the hospital for some tests. Is the girl inside the house your sister?”

“Yeah. Is she okay?”

“You should be with her. Call the hospital later for an update on your stepdad.”

“Thanks.” Levin left the ambulance and met Maggie in the front yard. They walked to the house together, careful to avoid the responders occupying the area. They reached the doorway, where Rana stood staring into the front room at the investigators working the scene.

Rana wrapped her arms around Levin and buried her face into his shoulder. He peered over her head and into the house to assess the situation: a thin spray of blood covered the wall and part of a picture, blood drops stained the carpet, and there was no other sign of his mother.

Walt wasn’t injured in a way that would do this. His mother could be trapped somewhere, bleeding to death.

He tried to clear the lump from his throat and focused on an officer, who seemed to recognize the pleading in his eyes. The officer approached the group.

“You must be the brother. I’m Officer Wyatt. The crime scene investigators arrived shortly before you did. We need to stay out of the room until they're through."

Levin tried to remain as calm as possible with his crying sister in his arms. "I understand. Do you know what happened?"

"Only pieces right now. We know someone, or some people, entered after 6:00. That's when Rana said she spoke to her mother about needing to work late at the store. We're treating the case as a missing person. Until we have reason to believe otherwise, that's how it will stay. We hope your stepdad can give us some information when he wakes up."

Levin watched the people in the room collect blood from the wall and floor with cotton swabs as he tried to piece together what happened.

The Project Renovatio people must have done this. But he'd thought Maggie was the one at risk, not his mother. What had he missed? Rana squeezed him tighter, and his shoulder became wet from her tears.

"Let's sit out front," Maggie said.

Rana finally released Levin, and they sat at the small patio set on the porch. The officer followed them outside, went to his car, and brought back three bottles of water. Rana couldn't open hers with her shaking hands. The officer took it and opened it for her. A young woman with long, blonde hair pulled into a ponytail came from inside the house and stood in the doorway. She held a piece of paper.

"Are you Levin?" she asked towards the group.

"I am. What's going on?" He rose from his chair and met her at the door.

"We found this on the couch, under a pillow. It has your name on it. I can't let you have it because it's evidence, but I thought you should see it. Maybe you can help us figure out what it means."

"Okay."

She held the unfolded yellow paper towards him so he could read the ten words written on it in blue ink:

You should have listened. Tell Maggie to watch her back.

Fury coursed through his body like lightning. He pounded the side of his fist against the doorframe. Clenching his jaw, he groaned and stared at the porch while he tried to form a thought.

"Sir? Are you all right?"

"I need a minute."

"Of course. Come find me inside." She left him by the doorway and re-entered the house.

He left the porch and stormed into the front yard, where he paced and weighed his options.

The police could find his mother eventually, but he figured the Project people knew how to keep the authorities away from their affairs. Waiting wasn't an option. He imagined a hypothetical scene, similar to the current one in the house, in which Maggie was the missing victim.

He froze in his tracks, looked at the night sky, and shouted in frustration.

Someone tapped the back of his arm. Rana stood next to him, and Maggie watched him from the porch.

He had to protect them. He pulled his phone from his pocket and accessed his contact list.

"Who are you calling?" Rana asked.

"Scott. He said to call him if PR caused any trouble."

"You think PR did this?"

The note's words replayed in his mind, and he nodded.

She squinted. "Doesn't Scott work for PR?"

He stopped scrolling. "We have to do something, and this is all I've got." He pressed the contact and held his phone to his ear.

Chapter Thirteen

Rana's ringtone jolted her into consciousness, and her heart raced when she didn't recognize her surroundings. The caller ID reminded her: she was at Levin's apartment. Maggie drove her here last night–or early this morning.

"Hello?" She couldn't hide the grogginess in her voice.

"I woke you. Sorry. I picked up Dayla from Alicia's house, and we're on our way to you." Levin's voice boomed through the phone.

"What time is it?" She searched for her phone to check the time before remembering she held it against her head.

"Almost 10:30. Did Maggie leave?"

Rana rose from the couch and wandered around his meticulously neat apartment. "I don't see her." She glanced outside. "Her car's not here."

"Good. I sent her . . . away. We'll get there in twenty minutes."

"Okay." She ended the call.

Twenty minutes. Plenty of time to take a shower.

She scanned the room for the backpack she'd hastily stuffed with clothes when the police told her she couldn't stay at her mother's house. It rested upside-down next to the front door.

While the water ran over her skin, she tried to sort out last night's events. Most of the images felt like a dream, as if she could go home and see her mom sitting at the table and drinking coffee. When she recalled the smaller details–her mom's voice during her last phone call, her panic when she saw the blood, the terror of thinking Walt had died–she found herself doing more crying than washing.

Keys jostled from the front door as she toweled off. Levin's voice came through the bathroom door, and Rana rushed to get dressed.

She emerged from the bathroom. Dayla sat on the couch, clutching her backpack and staring at the wall. Dayla made eye contact with Rana, dropped her backpack, and ran into Rana's open arms. Levin stood in the kitchen and talked on his phone. He still wore the cargo shorts and blue T-shirt he had on the night before.

"Levin said we can't go home." Dayla spoke into Rana's bicep, muffling her words.

"Yeah. Did he tell you why?"

"Something happened to Mom and Dad."

"That's right, but we don't know what yet. We're staying here until it's safe to go home."

Rana squeezed Dayla, thankful her sister hadn't seen the house.

Levin joined them. "That was a nurse at the hospital. Walt woke up. I'm going there now. You and Dayla stay here. Call work and tell them you're not coming in."

"I'm not scheduled today."

"Good. Just lay low. I brought in some groceries. Help yourself."

Dayla released herself from Rana's arms and entered the kitchen. The mention of food must have made her hungry.

Rana lowered her voice and stepped closer to Levin. "Have you slept?"

"No. I'm fine. I went back to the house this morning to let the cleaning people in." He put his hand on her shoulder and looked into her eyes. "How are you doing?"

Her eyes burned. "I'm scared," she said in a near whisper.

He pulled her close for a hug. "So am I." He released her, took her by the hand, and led her to the couch, where they sat facing each other. Dayla rejoined them, sat in a chair on the opposite side of the room, and peeled a banana. Rana considered sending her away again but decided she probably needed to know more of their situation. Her mother was missing, too. Still, Rana hoped her sister wasn't entirely listening.

"I've been up all night, partly because I had no choice, and partly because I've been thinking." Levin leaned closer to Rana and lowered his voice. "Do you remember what Scott said about why PR created us?"

"Yeah. To survive. We're supposed to be smarter and stronger and healthier than everyone else."

"Right. So, why don't we use that to find Mom? Or to fight PR? Or whatever we have to do? We can do things the police won't or can't do. I don't know about you, but I don't intend to sit back and wait to see if people who don't know our mom or our situation can find her."

"Okay. So what do we do?"

"I'm not sure yet. I'm going to visit Walt and see if he knows anything, and then I'm picking Scott up at the airport. I'll take him to the house to look for anything that will help us."

"Where's Maggie?"

"I sent her to her uncle's place in Arizona until I figure out what's going on and how to keep her safe."

"She left just because you told her to?"

Levin scowled. "Well, not *just* because I told her to. She wants to stay safe too. If anyone asks you–and I mean anyone–tell them we broke up and I don't know where she is."

"Even Scott?"

"Yeah. I'm not taking any chances. I'll call you later." He gave Rana a quick hug and stood. "Call me if you notice anything weird."

"Like what?"

"Anything."

****

After driving a few miles from his apartment, Levin turned his mother's phone back on, in case she needed to reach them and only knew her own number. Project Renovatio likely had her information, and he didn't want them tracking her phone and figuring out where he lived. His paranoia made him uncomfortable.

Part of him wished the police hadn't given the phone to him, but he couldn't have found Dayla without it.

He met two police officers at the hospital. They walked together to Walt's room, but Levin entered first, leaving the officers in the hall.

Walt lay in bed and stared out the window. His blond hair looked dirty, and he needed a shave. It occurred to Levin that he needed a shave, too, and he touched his jawline to confirm the presence of stubble.

"Hi, Walt," Levin said from the door.

Walt looked at him. "Levin. I…what…"

Levin entered the room and stood next to the bed. "Do you know why you're here?"

"The nurse said Rana found me passed out. She said someone drugged me," he said through an unusually scratchy voice.

"That's right. Did she tell you anything else?"

"No. Is your mom here?"

He took a deep breath. "No. She's missing."

"Missing?" Walt sat up.

"Yeah. When Rana got home from work last night, she found you on the floor and blood in the living room, but no sign of Mom. Rana called me, and I told her to call the police. They collected evidence. I have Mom's phone." He handed it to Walt.

"What am I supposed to do with this?"

"Answer it if someone calls, I guess. The police are in the hallway and want to talk to you."

"Oh. Sure."

Levin went to the hall to retrieve the officers, who followed him into the room. Levin sat in a chair by the window.

“Good morning, sir. I’m Officer Wyatt, and this is Officer Ortiz. We worked on your wife’s case last night. We’d like to ask you some questions, if that’s all right.”

“Okay.”

“Rana said she spoke to her mother on the phone around 6:00 yesterday afternoon. She came home from her job at the store at 11:20, when she found you and the evidence in the living room.”

Walt’s attention wandered; he stared at the wall behind Levin.

“Sir, are you okay?” Officer Wyatt asked.

“Oh, yeah. I’m listening.”

“Okay. Can you remember anything that happened at your house after Rana’s call? Anything at all?”

“Well, let’s see. Liz and I ate dinner around 6:30, I guess it was. Dayla stayed the night at a friend’s house. We put a movie on after dinner. I remember someone rang the doorbell in the middle of the movie…” His words trailed off and he went back to blankly staring at the wall.

“Walt, do you remember who came to the door?” Levin asked.

“I, um, no.” He squeezed his eyes closed. “I heard Liz yell.” He coughed as tears escaped. “I didn’t remember that before.” He brought his hand to his face and sobbed for a minute, pulled himself together, and continued. “I ran to see what happened, and a short guy with a ski mask on stuck a needle in my neck.” He moved his hand to his neck. “Here. I don’t remember anything after that. Next thing I know, I was waking up in here.”

"Do you remember looking out the front door? Did you see any vehicles? How many people entered your house?" Officer Ortiz asked in between taking notes.

"I dunno–two, maybe? I remember seeing another hooded guy in the front room before the short one got me." He paused again and stared at his feet. "I shoulda answered the door. I coulda protected her. I told her I would protect her."

"Protect her from what, sir?"

Walt looked to Levin, who took over, but cautiously. How much should he say? "My family is involved with a group–a research organization. They tried to be more invasive, so my mom sent them a letter telling them to back off. They threatened my girlfriend, but we didn't think they would come after us." Levin's emotions caught in his throat; he cleared it. "I broke up with Maggie last night and told her to leave the state for a while. I don't know where she went."

"I'm sorry to hear that. Is this group still a threat to her?" Officer Wyatt asked.

"No. They wanted me to break up with her from the beginning. They have what they want now."

"Seems like a lot of trouble for them to care about your love life. Do you know where they might have taken your mother?"

"We have the address where she sent the letter. It's probably in her email." He walked to Walt and took the phone. He searched on the touch screen before turning it around to the officers. "Here."

Officer Ortiz jotted it down. “San Diego? I’ll call the department to get someone to check it out.” He left the room.

Officer Wyatt’s gaze followed his partner out the door before he turned to Levin. “What kind of research does this group do?”

Levin swallowed, remembering Scott’s warning about the public’s likely response if they knew of the Project. A few awkward seconds passed before he answered. “It has to do with genetics. It’s kind of complicated.”

“Genetics? Like what? Cloning?”

Levin glanced at the door. “No, not cloning.” What would Scott say? Too many silent seconds passed for Levin to elaborate.

“So what do they do?”

Officer Ortiz re-entered the room and handed a card to Walt, interrupting Officer Wyatt’s line of questioning. “All right. Thanks for your time. We’ll contact you if we find anything or if we have more questions. Call us if you have any additional information. Oh, and what’s the name of the research organization?”

Levin sighed with relief at the safer question. “Project Renovatio.” The cops could ask PR directly about their research.

The officer wrote it down. “Thanks. I hope you get to feeling better,” he said to Walt. He turned his attention to Levin. “Can we speak to you in the hall?”

Levin held his breath, nodded, and followed them out of the room. They walked through the hallway towards the elevators, where they stopped and faced him.

"Sir," Officer Ortiz said, "can you tell us about the relationship between your mother and stepfather?"

Levin took a step back. "Uh, yeah, they get along all right."

"Do you think your stepfather would do anything to your mother?" Officer Wyatt asked.

"No, I don't think so. And besides, he was unconscious."

The officer nodded and wrote in the notebook. "And what about you? Do you have a good relationship with your mother?"

He leaned forward. "Are you suggesting I had something to do with this?"

"No, sir, we just need to eliminate all the incorrect possibilities. Most of the time, these cases lead us to someone in the family."

"My mother and I are fine. I love my family."

The officer wrote in his notebook again. "Okay. Thank you. Call me if there's anything else you can tell us." The officers turned around and walked into the elevator.

****

Scott appeared ready to get right to business when Levin arrived at the airport. He even dressed for the occasion, wearing Dockers, a burgundy golf shirt, and carrying a laptop case. "Tell me everything that's happened so far."

Levin described the events as he drove, looking at the road and occasionally glancing at Scott. "Well, when Rana got home from work late last night, she found Walt–my mom's husband–passed out on the floor. There was blood spray on the wall of the living room and blood on the carpet. She called me in a panic. I told her to call 9-1-1."

"You called the police?"

Levin scrunched his eyebrows. "Yeah. Seemed like the thing to do with a missing person and blood everywhere."

"All right. What else happened?"

"The police found a note. It said, 'You should have listened. Tell Maggie to watch her back.' That's when I called you."

"Where is Maggie now?"

Maggie was safe, but Levin paused as if holding back tears to make his lie more believable. He stared at the road. "I told her it wasn't safe for us to stay together, that I love her too much to put her at risk. I told her to leave the state for a while and not talk to me. I don't know where she went."

"That's good–for her, I mean. They'll probably leave her alone."

"I hope so."

"What about–Walt?"

"Yeah, Walt. He's okay. The kidnappers drugged him. He's still in the hospital." He looked at Scott. "Do you know where my mother is?"

"I'm afraid I don't. She may just appear somewhere, though, now that you've broken up with Maggie. Can I see your mother's house?"

"We're on our way there now."

"Okay. What information did you give the police about PR?"

Levin glanced at him. "I gave them the address my mother used to send the letter. I also told them the name."

"That won't get them anywhere. PR stays very underground. The address your mother used goes to a mailbox in a building we only use to collect mail. It's the same building I sent you to when you came to San Diego. No one's there except for the guard."

"Oh."

"And the name isn't written anywhere. Not even on checks. We use a dummy name."

"Why?"

"To keep people off our trail. Remember what I said about the general population not taking kindly to the work we do? The information you gave the police will lead to dead ends. I'll see what I can do to learn where your mother is. But I'll need to figure out a way to ask without actually asking so they don't know I'm working with you."

"Thanks."

Scott focused out the passenger window. "Do you ever wonder what the PR kids could do if they teamed up?"

"What do you mean?"

"You know, like on a sports team or something."

"Well, I don't think I'd bet against a team like that."

Scott laughed. "Or what if they joined the army? What if PR kids made up the whole army?"

"What are you talking about?"

"Nothing. Just something I thought about the other day."

Levin scowled in Scott's direction before turning his attention to the road.

They traveled another twenty minutes before arriving at Liz's house. When he unlocked the door, the smell of cleansers nearly overwhelmed him.

"I guess they did a good job." Levin coughed and scanned the living room. "I don't see any blood."

The investigators had found the note under a pillow. Levin flipped over all the pillows in a vain attempt to find something more. Scott entered the kitchen; Levin followed and found him standing in the middle of the room.

"What do you think?" Levin asked.

"It doesn't make sense. Why did they take your mother instead of Maggie to begin with? And if they kidnapped your mother to get to you, and now you've done what they want, shouldn't they have reason to, you know, give her back?"

"I think so."

"That hasn't happened. And they haven't said how you can get her back. We're missing something." He held his arm across his torso, supporting his elbow. His hand stroked his chin and he rocked on his feet. "Did your mom save a copy of the letter she sent, maybe in her email?"

"Yeah, I used it to find the address." Levin led Scott to the desk in the family room and opened the laptop. While it loaded, he studied the small cork board where his mother pinned various papers and fliers. Nothing seemed unusual.

The computer finished loading, and he opened his mother's email program. Three new emails had appeared since Levin used her phone, and one caught his attention.

Scott leaned over his shoulder. “That message has your name in the subject line.”

“I noticed.” Levin opened the message.

Levin,

You were foolish to think your mother could stop communicating with us. Before we tell you where she is, we want to know if you can follow directions, since you did not heed our warning about your girlfriend. Another PR family lives near you. Rana knows them, but only one in the family knows her. The walls tell the story. That family has your next step.

“No, not this clue nonsense again. Now they’re just screwing with us.” Levin placed his elbows onto the desk and his face in his hands before he remembered something. He spun the chair around to face Scott. “You left the clues last time.”

Scott shook his head. “It wasn’t only me. I was part of a group. The front man.”

“So you have nothing to do with this?” Levin raised his eyebrows. “It’s pretty convenient the clues appear the same time you do.”

“You called me, remember? I’m not involved this time. You’ll just have to trust me.”

They stared at each other. Levin clenched his jaw and faced the computer again. “We need to retrieve my sisters.”

“Yeah, I figured. Do you know who they’re talking about?”

“I think I do. But Rana needs to lead the way.”

Chapter Fourteen

After Levin printed the email, he and Scott returned to the car.

Levin started the engine. “Don’t you know the location of all the PR families?”

“No, I don’t. They tell me where to go and who to talk to as needed.”

“Of course they do.” He put his elbow on the window and rubbed his forehead with his thumb and finger. “Have you tried getting information from them yet?”

“No. But I figured out a way to do it.”

Scott retrieved his phone from his pocket and found a contact. He silently held his phone to his ear for a few seconds. “Hi. It’s Scott. One of my brothers contacted me saying something happened to his mom. Just wondering if you know anything about it. Call me back.”

“That was simple. Who’d you call?”

"My dad–Steven Craig. He knows I met with you, so he won't be surprised you called me. And he might know something."

They sat in silence for the remainder of the drive. Levin yawned as he pulled into his apartment complex and parked the car. "Wait here. I'll get the girls."

****

"What do you mean another family?" Rana rose from the couch and stood with one hand on her hip, glaring at her brother and refusing to believe the Project knew about the party.

"That's what the message said."

"Do we really have to go on another treasure hunt? Maybe the police will find Mom."

"I don't think so. I don't see another option."

Rana stewed for a moment. "Fine." She yelled into the bedroom. "Dayla, we're leaving."

Dayla tromped out of the room, holding a book. "I know; I heard you guys. You were loud enough."

"Sorry. Let's go." Rana put her arm around her sister's shoulders. Levin locked the door and led the way to the car.

"Is that Scott?" Dayla asked.

"Yeah. He's helping us find Mom." Levin took his place in the driver's seat while the girls piled into the back seat.

Scott twisted around. "Hello again, ladies. It's nice to see you."

"Hi," Dayla said. Rana picked at her fingernails and stared out the windshield.

Scott turned his attention to Levin. "My dad–Dr. Craig–called me back."

"And?"

"He told me to stay out of it."

"Well, there you go. I guess I didn't need to call you after all."

"No, it's fine. I'm hoping to pick up on patterns in case PR does this to another family."

"Do you think they will?"

"Can't say for sure. I hope they don't."

Rana directed Levin to Jason's house. She gritted her teeth and tried to decide how to explain herself. *I hear you belong to Project Renovatio, too!* Nope. *Can you tell me where your dad lives?* Terrible. *So, you come to this gene pool often?* Ugh.

Scott faced the back seat again. "How did you know they meant that family in the email?"

"I . . . um . . . saw Jason trip into the wall and dent it. *The walls tell the story*. I don't understand how they could have known that, though."

"Who did you tell about it?"

"Just my friend, Jacey, and Levin. But lots of other people came to the party. I suppose one of them could have said something to someone."

"Hmmm." Scott typed into his phone.

They arrived much sooner than Rana would have liked. Of course, if she had the choice, they wouldn't be there at all.

"What should I do? Go by myself?" she asked.

"No. I'll go with you. Dayla, stay in the car with Scott." Levin looked at Scott. "Is that okay?"

"Of course. She'll be fine." He smiled towards Dayla in the back seat.

Levin and Rana left the car, walked to the porch, and rang the doorbell. A tall woman with short, brown hair answered. She examined the two standing adjacent to each other on her porch.

"Hi . . . um, are you Mrs. Burke?" Rana asked.

"Yes. Can I help you?"

"I'm Rana Davis. I go to school with Jason. This is my brother, Levin."

"Oh, how nice. Would you like me to get him for you?" She turned and pointed up the stairs.

"No, thank you. I actually need to ask you a question. It's gonna sound kinda weird."

Mrs. Burke shifted her feet and crossed her arms. "Okay. Go ahead."

"Does the name 'Project Renovatio' mean anything to you?"

Mrs. Burke's jaw dropped. She gently pushed them outside and closed the door behind her. "How do you know about that?" She glared at Rana.

"We're part of it."

Mrs. Burke glanced at the closed door. "Jason doesn't know about Project Renovatio. He thinks my husband is his biological father." She looked at the car. "Can I ask what's going on here?"

Rana's eyes burned as she fought back tears. The idea that she and Jason were alike overwhelmed her. She stared at Levin, hoping he would take over the explanation.

He nodded. "Yes, ma'am. Someone kidnapped our mother last night. PR is behind it–it's a long story. Anyway, they said we'd find her when we follow a set of directions. The first one suggested you have the next clue we need."

Mrs. Burke looked past them for a moment before her eyes widened. "Oh my goodness. Wait here a minute." She went back into the house, then reappeared holding a blue envelope.

"I found this under my windshield wiper. It doesn't mean anything to me; I put it into our recycling bin. Maybe it will mean something to you." She handed it to Levin.

He opened the envelope and removed a yellow paper with a message written on it in blue ink. Rana read the message to herself.

Now you must go to the Paddle Dog Motel.

"What's the Paddle Dog Motel?" she asked Levin.

"I have no idea." He faced Mrs. Burke. "Thank you. This looks like what we need."

"I'm glad. I hope you find your mother safe, and soon. I must say, I'm disturbed the Project would do something like this. Should I be concerned?"

"I don't think so. This was personal. We'll call if you need to know more."

"I appreciate that. I'll let you be on your way." She re-entered the house, and the siblings returned to the car.

****

Levin's stomach turned when he saw the yellow paper–identical to the one the investigator showed him the night before. He kept the discovery to himself, as Rana didn't need another reason to stress.

When they re-entered the car, both Dayla and Scott looked at them expectantly. Levin read the note aloud.

"What's the Paddle Dog Motel? Sounds like a fancy pet boarding place," Scott said.

Levin shrugged, pulled his phone from his pocket, and did a search for the name. “Nothing’s coming up here.”

“Can I see the note?” Dayla held her hand toward the front seat.

“Sure, I guess.” He gave it to her.

She held it with both hands over her lap and examined it. “Does anyone have a pencil?”

“Why?” Levin asked.

“I want to see something.”

“Okay.” He opened the glove compartment in front of Scott and jostled its contents. “I have a pen. Will that work?”

“Yeah.”

He handed her the pen and watched her write. She drew lines from *Paddle Dog Motel* and wrote the letters in different orders beneath it.

“You think it’s an anagram?” Rana asked.

“Yep. ‘Paddle Dog Motel’ is meaningless. So the real meaning is hidden.”

Scott smiled at Dayla. “You’re very smart.”

“Thank you,” she said without looking up from the paper. Scott chuckled.

Levin pulled the car into the street. “I need coffee, and it’s almost dinnertime. Let’s see if Dayla can figure that out before I get to a restaurant. Loser pays for dinner.”

Dayla grinned at him and went back to writing on the paper. “Everyone, be quiet.”

He laughed to himself. Five minutes into the drive, worry filled his gut.

What if she couldn't figure it out? They'd be stuck with this meaningless message and no other clues to follow.

As Levin drove into the parking lot of a fast food place, Dayla asked, "Does 'gold plated dome' mean anything?"

"Maybe. The capitol building downtown has a gold-plated dome," Rana said.

"I guess you win." Levin faced the back seat and winked at Dayla.

****

Rana had to admit the clues provided a welcome distraction from last night's traumas, though unease took hold in her gut when she considered how close whoever took her mother must be to leave the clues. She didn't voice her concern in case no one shared it.

They arrived at the capitol building as the sun lowered behind the mountains. Levin found a spot on a side street to park the car, and the group walked together to the building. Rana glared at Scott. Why did he join them? He didn't contribute much to their efforts, and he worked on his phone constantly.

Rana pointed to the top of the building. "See, Dayla? That's the gold-plated dome. It's covered with thin sheets of real gold."

"Cool." Dayla scanned the rest of the building. "What are we looking for?"

Levin strolled towards the building's front steps. "I'm not sure. I guess we should walk around and search for something meaningful." He jogged up the steps, tried one of the doors, and found it locked. He turned and examined the tall arches guarding the entryway. The rest joined him, scanning different parts of the building.

"What's that?" Rana pointed to a small blue square taped to the inside of one of the arches about ten feet above the ground.

"I don't know, but it looks out of place." Levin jumped, trying to grab it. After three attempts, he searched for another solution. "Dayla, come here and sit on my shoulders."

He crouched so she could climb on, and he held her legs as he returned to standing. When he swerved to adjust her weight, Dayla yelled and grabbed his hair.

"Ow! I've got you. Don't do that."

She giggled. "Sorry."

Levin stood close to the arch while Dayla reached up and grabbed the blue square. "It's an envelope." She pulled the tape from the surface, handed it to Rana, and climbed down from Levin's shoulders.

Rana opened the envelope, removed a yellow paper, and read aloud, "There is a tower at the corner of Arapahoe and 16th. There is a backpack on the park side of the tower. Your clue is inside, along with a dye pack set to burst at 8:30. You might want to run."

Rana yanked her phone from her pocket and checked the time. "It's 8:21." She accessed her GPS and entered the intersection. "It's just over a mile away." She dropped the envelope and paper and darted away.

"Rana," Levin yelled, but she didn't look back.

She ran as fast as her legs allowed towards the tower, wishing she had worn her sneakers. She never ran track while wearing flip-flops. When she turned onto 16th Street, she froze to take in the number of people on the sidewalk. No cars drove on the street. Instead, a single bus lane ran in each direction to transport those who didn't want to walk.

She ran on the bus route running opposite of her direction, jumping onto the sidewalk to let busses pass. She only slowed when cars at cross streets forced her to do so.

Tightness gripped her chest after half a mile of sprinting, but she didn't relent. When she hopped onto the sidewalk, her sandal caught the curb, and she couldn't recover her balance. Pain shot through her arm as she skidded to a stop on the sidewalk. A few bystanders gathered around her, but she jumped to her feet and resumed her run, though slower from the limp she now had.

The tower grew larger. She gave a new burst of speed to her effort in spite of the pain in her ankle. She glanced at her phone to check the time: 8:28.

Panting, she rounded the corner of the tower and spotted a black backpack against the wall. A popping sound came from it in the same moment.

"No!"

She rushed to it, fell to her knees, and yanked the zipper open, knowing what she would see but still nervous to discover the contents. A paper sat in the middle of a mess of red ink.

Slumping over the backpack, she cried as Levin's car stopped on the curb near her.

****

Levin found his sister hunched over a backpack next to the tower. Her back heaved with shaking breaths.

She didn't make it.

He ran to her, kneeled, and put his arm around her. She flinched.

He pulled back and moved to her other side. A large, bleeding scrape covered much of her upper arm and shoulder. “What the hell happened to you?”

“It’s okay.” She wiped her tears with the back of her hand.

“No, it looks awful.”

She lifted the open backpack. “I was too late.”

He swallowed the lump in his throat. “Let’s take it with us. Maybe we can wipe enough off before it dries.” He helped Rana to her feet and led her to the car. He opened the trunk in search of something he could ruin and found a T-shirt his company gave him at a fundraiser.

Scott and Dayla joined them at the trunk. Levin pulled the paper from the backpack and wrapped it in the shirt. Scott held a bottle of water over Levin’s shoulder and asked, “Will this help?”

Levin wiped the paper with no effect. “It’s worth a shot.” He poured water on the shirt and wiped the paper again. The water smeared the ink but didn’t allow him to see any writing. He slumped, then returned the paper to the backpack. He used the un-inked part of the shirt to clean Rana’s injury.

“Rana, what happened to your arm?” Dayla asked.

“It’s okay. I fell. I would have made it in time if I stayed on my feet.” She stared at the backpack through every word.

“You can’t blame yourself,” Scott said. “The Project did this. They didn’t have to take it this far.”

Levin twisted around and connected with Scott's eyes. "I hope you're not planning to continue working for them."

Scott pursed his lips and looked at Levin without replying.

Rana sighed. "Now what do we do?"

"We go home. We'll hope for a new lead tomorrow." Levin couldn't ignore his developing headache, likely a symptom of staying awake for thirty-six straight hours.

Everyone loaded into the car. Rana and Dayla fell asleep on the way to their mother's house.

Chapter Fifteen

"Scott, what's your plan?" Levin drove towards his apartment after leaving the girls with Walt at his mother's house.

"I'm going back to San Diego in the morning. I can't do anything here to help you. I can do more there." Scott scrolled through his phone.

"Like what?"

"Go through files. Talk to people who might know something. I'll call you if I learn anything useful. I bought a plane ticket on our way to your mother's house. I'll take a cab to the airport in the morning. Do you mind if I stay at your apartment tonight?"

"No. As long as you don't mind sleeping on a couch."

They rode in silence the rest of the way. As Levin unlocked his door, he received a text. Once inside, he checked it; Maggie's name lit the screen. He suppressed a grin so Scott wouldn't get suspicious.

"You can get a blanket from the closet and extra towels from under the sink in the bathroom. Help yourself to whatever you want in the kitchen. Do you need anything else?" Levin stepped towards his room.

"No, thanks. I brought some things with me."

"Okay. I'm exhausted. I'll see you in the morning." Levin retreated to his room. With the door closed behind him, he pulled his phone from his pocket and read her message again.

I miss you.

He smiled. *I miss you, too. Did you get there okay?*

I did. It's hot here. How long do I have to stay?

I don't know. We had a setback tonight. Hoping to get back on track tomorrow. He wished he could answer differently. He wasn't going to let her return until he found his mother, and even then, they'd need to find somewhere else to live. *I wish you were here.*

Me too. I love you.

I love you, too.

****

The next morning, Rana woke in her own bed and scanned her room. Dayla slept on the floor, wrapped in a blanket that covered everything but her hair.

Checking her alarm clock, Rana decided it wasn't too early to get up. Dayla must have sensed movement, because she stirred and sat up.

"Hey, girlie. What are you doing on my floor?"

"I got scared last night. I remembered Mom isn't here."

Rana crouched to Dayla's level and hugged her. "Your dad's here."

"I know." Dayla stretched and moaned. "Do you think we'll find her today?"

"I hope so. Let's get breakfast."

The girls walked downstairs. Walt sat at the table, drinking from a coffee mug. He appeared clean and shaved again.

"Good morning, girls," he said after taking a sip.

"Hi," Rana said. "How are you feeling?"

"I'm okay. I want to get your mother back. I remembered something in the middle of the night and called the police. They're headed here now."

"What did you remember?" Rana asked, desperate for any new information.

"You can sit with me when I talk to them. Dayla, I want you to go upstairs when they get here."

"Okay." She seemed used to people sending her away.

The girls poured bowls of cereal for themselves as a knock sounded from the front door.

"They're here." Walt walked to the door to greet them. Dayla took her cereal upstairs. Rana ate hers at the table and waited.

As they came in, Rana recognized one of the officers from the night her mom disappeared.

"Hi, Rana. I don't know if you remember me. I'm Officer Wyatt."

"You gave me the bottle of water."

"That's right. How have you been doing?"

Telling them about the clues PR left could make them stop leaving any clues at all, so she answered generically. "I'm better. Do you know anything about my mom?"

"Not much. The information your brother gave us didn't get us anywhere. The address your mom used to send the letter belongs to an empty building." He studied Rana for a moment. "Is there anything else you need to tell us about the research organization?"

"I don't think so." She shoved another bite of cereal into her mouth.

He pursed his lips. "Okay." He turned his attention to Walt. "Sir, you said you remembered something last night."

"Yeah. Liz ripped the hood off the guy who grabbed her."

Rana nearly spit the cereal across the table. "What? How did you not remember that before?" She glared at Walt as she used the back of her hand to wipe away the milk dribbling down her chin.

"It's not surprising, miss. The drugs they shot into his neck probably gave him short-term amnesia of the events immediately before the injection. The smaller details return over time," the other officer said.

Walt turned his attention to the cops. "I remember being surprised because the guy looked like Levin. It was after the short guy drugged me. I thought it was Levin for a second, 'til he yelled at Liz. His voice was different."

Rana stared at Walt and blinked a few times. "Are you sure? Maybe you had a dream about what happened."

"No, I'm certain."

Rana ran upstairs to grab her phone.

****

Levin called work and told them he wouldn't be in for a few days. *It could be quite a few days*, he thought. He still held his phone when it rang.

"Hey. How's your arm?"

"Two cops are here. Walt called them. He said Mom took the hood off the guy who grabbed her, and the guy looked like you."

"What? That doesn't make sense." Would any of his brothers do something like that? And why? Scott wasn't in Denver until the next day. Jeremy had darker skin, a detail Walt probably would have mentioned. That left Brent and Daniel. But Walt had met Brent. Wouldn't he recognize Brent after just two weeks? Maybe not, if Brent was in a struggle with their mother and Walt was watching from a distance.

"Rana, ask Walt if the guy said anything."

"He did. He said he thought the guy was you until he yelled at Mom. His voice was different."

"He didn't say anything about a stammer?"

"No. Hold on, I'll go ask."

The phone went quiet, and Levin remembered Brent's friendly yet shy demeanor, one Levin wouldn't associate with someone harboring a desire to threaten and kidnap people. If Brent planned and executed this, he'd done an impressive job of fooling everyone.

A second later, Rana came back on the line. "He said he didn't, but the guy only yelled, like, four words. One of the officers wants to talk to you."

Before Levin said anything, someone with a deep voice spoke into Rana's phone. "Sir, this is Officer Wyatt. It sounds like you might know the guy who took your mom. I need you to tell me his name."

"I don't know, exactly." He stood and paced around his room. "I have some half-brothers who look like me. I've narrowed it to two possibilities, but I don't know why either of them would want to kidnap my mother."

"We'll worry about that later. Right now, I need their names, addresses, phone numbers, and anything else you can tell me."

Levin relayed the information he had for Brent and Daniel. He made a mental note to call them himself later.

Rana's voice came through the phone. "I don't think it was Brent. We've emailed a few times. He doesn't do anything that interesting."

"I don't think it's him either, but we could be wrong. We haven't known him that long."

"But why would he–or the other brother–do this? What do they have to gain?"

He rubbed his neck. "I have no idea."

Chapter Sixteen

Scott had left by the time Levin emerged from his room. After Levin showered and shaved, he sent a text.

Are you at the airport?

Several minutes passed without a response. Levin grew impatient and went to his car to head to Liz's house. On the way, he got a call from a number he didn't recognize.

"Hello?"

"Levin? It's Daniel. In Oklahoma City."

"Oh. Hi." Levin racked his mind for what to say next. "What's going on?"

"Why don't you tell me?" He sounded angry. "The cops just called. They said your mother is missing and they wanted to question me."

Levin winced. "What did they want to know?"

"My whereabouts on Saturday night. That's about it. What is this?"

Levin told Daniel about the kidnapping and how Walt said one of the guys looked like him. "The cops are just eliminating possible suspects."

"Are they checking out the other guys too?" His tone sounded more curious than angry now.

"Just you and Brent. Scott flew into Denver the next morning. Jeremy has darker skin, which Walt didn't notice. I haven't talked to Brent yet. It could be a coincidence."

"What could?"

"That the kidnapper looks like us."

"That would be a hell of a coincidence."

Levin couldn't argue with his point.

"There's something else. It might not matter in your case, but I want you to know about it," Daniel said.

"Okay." Levin shifted in his seat.

"My family got a letter from Project Renovatio requesting we go to San Diego for some testing."

"Really? What kind of testing?"

"Genetic testing. It said they have a concern about a serious problem associated with one of the genes they manipulated. They want to treat us if we have that gene."

"What kind of problem?" Maybe Rana's concern about medical issues was a valid one.

"Some kind of blood problem. I don't know exactly. Anyway, my mom freaked and arranged for me to take Janie and get checked out. We have an appointment on Tuesday. PR paid for the airline tickets."

Levin couldn't decide what to make of the new information. "Do you think everyone got the letter?"

"No idea. It might be a gene from our mother and not concern you at all."

"Yeah. Okay. Thanks for letting me know. Sorry about the police getting in your business."

"It's no big deal. I hope you find your mom soon."

By the time the call ended, Levin had arrived at his mother's house. He called Brent before going inside.

It rang five times and went to a generic voicemail greeting. He hung up without leaving a message, went inside, and found his sisters watching TV in the family room. He took the opportunity to check his mom's email again.

****

After the police left, Rana called her store and told her boss about her situation. He gave her the week off. She needed it to find her mom and deal with PR, but part of her wished it hadn't delayed her car savings plan. That part filled her with guilt. Her mother could be trapped somewhere, bleeding or getting an infection, and here she was worried about a stupid car.

Pain radiated from her arm and ankle. She tried not to think about it, because whenever she did, she found herself examining the ink-covered paper from the backpack. She could barely read one word through the ink. *Alone*. It meant nothing, but she couldn't stop looking at it.

She folded the paper and returned it to her pocket before heading downstairs, where Dayla sat on the floor, watching a nature show on TV. She sat next to her sister. A few minutes later, Levin came in and did something on the computer.

"What are you doing?" Rana asked.

"Checking Mom's email, in case there's another clue." He closed the browser, revealing a picture of his sisters displayed on his mother's computer desktop. "Rana, did you say you emailed Brent?"

"Yeah. I haven't checked my email for a couple days."

"Why don't you check it? Maybe Brent sent you something. I can't reach him."

"Okay."

Levin removed himself from the desk chair, and Rana took his place while he stood behind her to see the screen. She opened her email and found two new messages; one showed Brent's name.

"There." Levin tapped the screen.

"I know; I can see it." She opened the message. Brent wrote about his job, and he answered questions about his family she had asked in her last message. One part caught her attention as being out of place. She read it aloud. "We received a letter from PR saying there might be a problem with our genes, like something might have gone wrong when they modified the DNA. I'm worried about my brother, so I'm taking him to San Diego on Monday. They want to do some kind of testing. Did you get a letter like this?"

"Daniel said his family got a letter like that from PR too. He thought the genetic problem came from their mom." Levin crossed his arms. "But that can't be, if Brent got the letter. When did he send this message?"

Rana checked the screen. "Saturday morning."

"And Mom disappeared Saturday night. Brent's going to San Diego today." He sat in the chair near the computer desk, and Rana spun the desk chair around to face him. "So let's pretend Brent abducted Mom. He sent you this message, came here that night with someone else to take her somewhere, and then went back to Seattle to take his brother to San Diego?"

"Maybe he isn't taking his brother to San Diego. Maybe he sent this to make us think that."

Levin shook his head. "No. Daniel getting the same letter is too much of a coincidence. I don't think Brent came here."

"So, who did?"

"I don't know. Where's the mail?"

Rana pulled a stack of unopened envelopes from a caddy on the desk and handed them to Levin.

He flipped through the envelopes and pulled one from the stack. "This one has my name on it and no stamp." He showed her the envelope and gave her the others to put back in the caddy. He pulled a yellow paper from the envelope and read the message aloud. "*You should follow your brothers.*"

Rana huffed. "That's messed up! Whoever took Mom left that here when they took her, knowing we would find it."

"I agree. I'll try calling Scott again." Levin held his phone against his head for a minute and returned it to his pocket after he didn't get an answer.

"So, what should we do?" she asked.

"Make plans to go to San Diego, I guess. We'll leave tonight."

****

Levin returned to his apartment to take a nap and prepare for the overnight drive. As he dozed, he imagined a hooded kidnapper gingerly placing the envelope among the other pieces of mail. How long had he thought it would take them to find it? What if they hadn't found it?

A text alert on his phone woke him. Scott's name lit the screen.

In San Diego. You'll never guess who's here.

Levin grinned as he typed his response.

Brent? He held his grin, waiting for Scott's reply.

You guessed correctly.

He laughed. *Any other PR kids there?*

A few. I guess they're calling some in for testing.

That's why Brent's there. Daniel's not far behind. We got another clue about Mom.

What was it?

A note saying I should follow my brothers. The girls and I are leaving tonight.

Scott's next message appeared after a long pause. *Okay. I'll look for you tomorrow. No new leads here.*

Levin wasn't surprised. For a guy who worked for PR, Scott seemed to know very little. He likely had his job because Dr. Craig raised him.

Levin sat up in bed and sent a text to one more person before packing his things.

How are you doing today? A gentle nervousness occupied his stomach as he waited for Maggie's reply.

I'm anxious to go home.

He sighed and wished he could call her. They had both decided to text because they could delete their conversations without anyone recording anything.

I know. I'm taking the girls to San Diego tonight. Mom might be there.

Really? Let me know when you find her.

I will. Then we can figure out where to go next. Excitement coursed through his body when he recalled Maggie agreeing to move somewhere for him.

I can't wait. See you soon.

****

"Hurry up, Dayla," Rana yelled into her sister's room.

"I am! How long will we be gone?"

"I don't know. Pack for a week."

She left Dayla alone and went to the back porch. Walt sat in a lawn chair facing the yard.

"Hey." She sat in the chair next to him.

"Oh, hey."

"How's it going?"

"I was just wondering what your mother's thinking right now. I hope she knows we have the police looking for her."

Rana smirked. Walt didn't realize she and her siblings were also looking for their mother. "Levin's driving us to San Diego. We leave in half an hour."

"Oh? What for?"

How should she explain this? "We think there's something that will help us find Mom."

He sat up. "Really? What?"

"We don't know yet."

He focused on her. "All right. I'm sure you kids know what you're doing."

"I hope so."

They sat in silence for a minute.

"Does Dayla know about the Project?" he asked.

Rana shook her head. "She doesn't know you're not her biological father. But she might have to find out soon."

He nodded, then squeezed his eyes closed.

She stood to go inside, glancing at Walt as she rose from her chair. She leaned over and put her arm around the back of his shoulders, giving him a side hug. He patted her hand. She released him and walked towards the house.

"Rana?"

She turned around. He had turned in his chair to face her. "I'm sorry . . . I'm sorry I wasn't really there for you kids before. And I'm sorry you had to find what you found the other night."

She smiled gently at him. "It's okay. I don't blame you for what happened."

His eyes welled with tears, and he turned to face the yard.

****

Levin entered his mother's house to collect his sisters. They met him at the door holding their duffel bags. The similarity of this moment to the first time they traveled to San Diego struck him.

"Do you have everything?" he asked.

"I think so. I told Walt where we're going."

He hadn't considered telling Walt. "Oh. That's good. Did he say anything?"

"He knows we want to find Mom."

He nodded and held the door open for them. They waited at the back of his car for him to open the trunk. With everything loaded and everyone settled, they started their trip.

"It seems strange to do this again. A month feels like a long time ago," Rana said as Levin entered the highway.

"Yeah. I know. A lot has changed."

"Remember what it felt like to be normal, like everyone else?"

Levin started to answer when Dayla interrupted. "Like everyone else? What are you talking about?"

He stole a glance at the back seat. Dayla was staring at him.

She needed to know more about their situation. Levin couldn't guess what they would find and have to explain in San Diego, and it would be easier to tell her here, with only the three of them. He sighed in an attempt to squelch the irritation that accompanied the necessity of the conversation.

"Okay, Dayla. I'll tell you. But I need to ask you a question first."

"Okay."

"What do you know about our dad? Mine and Rana's?"

"He died in a car accident when Mom was pregnant with Rana."

Rana twisted around in her seat, facing Dayla. "Well, that's not true. Our dad isn't dead." She glanced at Levin before returning her attention to her sister. "And Walt isn't your father. He's your stepdad, the same as he is to me and Levin."

"He's not?" Silence filled the car for several seconds, until Dayla broke it. "If he's not my dad, then who is? And where's your dad?" She gasped. "Do we have the same dad?"

"No, we don't." Rana wrapped her arm around the headrest. "The thing is, we're special. Do you remember learning about heredity in school?"

"Yeah. Kids look like their parents because the parents pass genes to them."

"Right. Kids get genes from their moms and dads. We all have features that came from Mom. You have her nose." Rana tapped her sister on the nose to make her smile. "I have her eyes. And we all have features that came from our dads, too."

"I bet your dad has black hair."

Levin laughed. "He probably does. He lives in Greece. We think he has black hair and olive skin, like mine."

"In Greece?" Dayla sat quietly for a moment. "Where's my dad?"

Rana locked the door and leaned against it. "He lives in Scotland. Some scientists took the best genes from him, and they took the best genes from Mom, and they combined them to make you. They designed us to be really smart, strong, and healthy."

Levin made eye contact with Dayla in the rear view mirror. "Do you think it worked?" He winked at her, and she giggled.

"Yeah," she said through her giggles. She didn't ask any more questions for several minutes. "Is that why Brent is your brother, too? Because he has the same dad as you?"

Rana smiled. "That's right. And you know what? You probably have other brothers and sisters too. You might even get to meet them."

Dayla didn't respond, and Levin checked the mirror. She stared out the window.

That was as much as she needed to know about Project Renovatio.

Chapter Seventeen

As Levin drove out of Las Vegas the next morning, he received a phone call from the police. He smiled, nodded, and said, "That's wonderful news"–the opposite of how Rana expected him to react to anything the police had to say.

Her heart swelled, hoping for good news. The instant he ended the call, she asked, "Did they find her?"

He shook his head. "They processed the blood from the living room. It all came from a single male subject."

Male subject? She sat up straighter. "So it wasn't Mom's."

"Exactly." He glanced out the side window, blinked rapidly and exhaled.

"And it means she fought them. Go Mom!" Tears welled in Rana's eyes.

"Why are you crying?" Dayla asked.

"Because I'm relieved. And proud. Mom's probably not hurt, and she can hold her own. She just needs to sit tight until we find her." Rana smiled at her sister and ruffled the girl's hair. Dayla scowled and fixed her hair.

They arrived in San Diego in time for lunch and stopped at a fast food place. When he finished eating, Levin stepped outside the restaurant to call Scott and find out where he should go. He re-entered looking confused.

"Well?" Rana asked through a mouthful of French fries. Dayla climbed around in the restaurant's play area.

"Remember the building we first went to last time? That's where Mom sent the letters. Scott said it was empty, but now they're using some of the space for the genetic testing. We're supposed to return to that building."

"Huh. Kinda seems like we're walking into something, doesn't it?"

"Well, yeah, we'll be walking into a building." Levin smirked at her.

"Ha ha. I mean, we're just letting Scott tell us where we should go. What if that isn't smart?"

"I think we can trust Scott. He said he'd meet us there."

She stared at him. "Okay." Her gut told her something wasn't right, but she didn't argue with her brother.

****

Fifteen minutes later, Levin drove towards the industrial area where they last found the building. He had a moment of déjà vu when he pulled up to the booth housing the same grumpy guard. Levin even offered the same greeting. “I’m here to meet Scott Miles.”

The guard referenced his clipboard. “Go right when you get into the parking lot. You’ll enter through those doors.” He pointed.

“Thanks.” Levin raised his window and drove into the lot. As he parked, he drummed his fingers on the steering wheel. “This doesn’t feel right.”

“I thought the same thing.” Rana sat up. “What should we do?”

Levin pulled his phone from his pocket and called Scott.

“Levin. Are you here?”

“Yeah. We’re in front of the building. Does anything inside seem fishy to you?”

“What do you mean?”

“I’m not sure.” He pressed his lips. “Something just feels off.”

“I wouldn’t worry. Brent, Daniel, and Jeremy are here with their siblings. The repeat performance of talking to the guard probably made you unsettled.”

“Jeremy’s there?”

“Yes. He arrived after we last spoke.”

Levin sighed. “All right. We’ll be in shortly.” He ended the call.

“So?”

“So, we don’t have another option. All of our brothers are here. The note said to follow them. I don’t see another way of finding Mom.” He examined the building.

“Levin, what’s wrong?” Dayla asked.

He shook his head. “Nothing. Let’s go.”

****

They entered the building and walked into a small room containing four elevators. One of them opened, and Scott stepped out.

"Hi, Levin." He shook Levin's hand. "I pulled some files for us to look at. They're in a room upstairs."

"Thanks, but I'd like to talk to our brothers first."

"Sure. I can take you to them." He entered the elevator. Levin and his sisters followed. The building had three floors and a basement. Scott pushed the button for the third floor.

"Daniel said the Project paid for him and his sister to come here," Levin said, more as small talk than as a push for information.

"Yes. I'm surprised you didn't get a letter. I can't figure out why you didn't."

"Maybe they used our missing mom to get us here," Rana quipped.

The doors on the opposite side of the elevator opened, and Scott led them down the hall. He entered what looked like a conference room: it contained three couches, some chairs, a refrigerator, a coffee table, and a TV. Levin's brothers and their siblings occupied the space. Scott walked across the room and sat on the couch next to a teenage boy with tan skin.

Brent smiled and approached them as they stood in the doorway. "Levin. I'm h…h…happy you're here. Hi, Rana."

"Hey, Brent. I just got your email yesterday. It's good to see you."

Brent waved a tall teenage boy with lighter brown hair over to the group. "This is mmmm…my b…brother, Isaiah." Isaiah shook hands with the three siblings, who introduced themselves. "We stayed in a mmm…motel last night. Mmm…maybe you guys can stay there, too."

Levin nodded. "Yeah, maybe. We haven't figured out where we're staying yet."

Brent grinned.

The group entered the room. Levin walked with his sisters to his other brothers. They each introduced themselves and their siblings to Rana and Dayla. Dayla's face brightened when Daniel introduced her to Janie. They sat together in one of the chairs and flipped through the books Dayla brought in her backpack. Soon, the girls were laughing and sharing about their schools and friends.

Levin approached Jeremy at his first opportunity. "Can I talk to you alone?"

"Sure." Jeremy turned away from him. "Scott, can Levin and I use the empty room across the hall to have a private conversation?"

"Yeah. There's no furniture, though."

"That's okay. We'll sit on the floor," Levin said. The men walked to the other room and sat against the wall farthest from the door.

Levin started right away with his concern. "I'm surprised to see you here."

"I'm sure you are. My family received the same letter that Daniel's and Brent's families received. I wanted to bring Eliot here for the testing."

"I figured. I really want to know about…" He paused to scan the room, saw nothing, but leaned in and dropped his voice to a whisper anyway. "I want to know about your fiancée."

"Yes. Renee. We are doing well. We haven't had any interference from the Project. My mom hasn't even stopped talking to them."

"That doesn't make sense. My mom wrote a letter cutting off communication, and some guys from the Project kidnapped her a couple weeks later. I sent my girlfriend to Arizona because they threatened her."

Jeremy's jaw dropped. "Are you serious? I'm so sorry."

"Thanks. But now I'm confused. Our mother is still missing. We're here because the Project left clues for us, and the last one said to follow my brothers. So here we are."

"I don't know what to say. That's terrible. Can I do anything to help?"

"I don't think so. I guess we can go back to the others." Levin dug his nails into his palm. Doing nothing instead of having his mother sever communication with the Project meant he could still be with Maggie.

The men rejoined the group. Scott had left the room.

"Scott said to wait here and someone would come get us when it's time for the testing," Daniel said.

"We're not here for the testing." Levin stared out the window. "I need to look around. Rana, stay here with Dayla."

Levin walked through the short hall and found each room empty. He turned the other way and found more empty rooms and a restroom. With nowhere else to go on that floor, he returned to his siblings.

"This is the only room with anything in it," he said.

Daniel peered down the hallway. “Weird.”

****

Everyone waited for over an hour, but the time passed quickly for the newly acquainted siblings. No employees came to the room. Rana grew impatient and left her place among the other teenagers to talk to Levin.

“Why are we still here? We should look for Mom.”

“I know. I just don’t know where to start.” Levin pursed his lips. “Maybe the three of us should search the rest of the building ourselves.”

“Anything’s better than sitting here waiting for nothing to happen.” She turned to the chair where Dayla and Janie sat. “Come on, Dayla. We’re going for a walk.”

The siblings walked into the hall, but this time they returned to the elevator. The second floor appeared identical to the third floor: empty rooms, a bathroom, and one room with furniture. Another group of people waited in that room. Rana peeked in, and Jason made eye contact with her. She gasped.

“What are you doing here?” she asked as she entered the room. Besides Jason, she didn’t recognize anyone. Levin and Dayla stood in the doorway.

Jason rose from the couch. “My sister and I came here for genetic testing. After you left my house the other day, my mom went through the mail from last week and found a letter about it.”

“You know I came to your house?”

“Yeah. She told me.”

“Is she here?” Rana scanned the room again.

"No. She couldn't get off work." He picked at his fingernails. "She told me about Project Renovatio and why she had me. I wondered if I'd see you here."

Rana got the impression he had more to say. "What do you think about the Project?"

"I'm angry. My whole life until now has been a lie. I don't even know my real father."

"Your mom said you thought her husband was your father. Maybe you can still think of him that way, since he raised you?"

"I dunno." He sighed. "My real father is some Scottish guy I'll never meet."

"He's Scottish?" Rana closely analyzed Jason's features, then looked at her sister. "Dayla, come here a second."

Dayla left the doorway and walked to Rana, who grabbed the girl's shoulders and positioned her beside Jason. Levin entered the room and stood next to Rana.

"Oh, my gosh." Rana brought her hand to her mouth. Dayla and Jason shared eye shape, hair color, height, and even freckle distribution. "This is too bizarre."

"What?" Jason asked.

"I think you two have the same father."

Dayla and Jason faced each other. Jason squinted a bit. "Huh. Mallory, come here."

A younger girl approached the group. Jason positioned her next to Dayla. The girls bore strong similarities as well.

"Mallory and I have the same father," Jason said.

"Um, wow. So I guess this answers the 'will we ever go out' question, seeing as you're my sister's brother." Rana giggled awkwardly.

"Yeah, I guess so." Jason laughed. "Wow. That sounds really bad. You don't..." he pointed from Rana to Dayla, "...have the same father too, do you?"

"No. My father is Greek."

A smile took over Jason's face. "Good. I was about to puke."

Rana laughed.

Levin cleared his throat, breaking the awkward pause. "Well, this has been educational, but we need to go." He motioned for the door.

"You're here for the testing, right?" Jason asked.

Rana shook her head. "Did your mom tell you why we went to your house?"

"Yeah. She said something happened to your mom."

"Right. We think she's here."

"Really? I hope you find her. You know," he turned his attention to Dayla, "everyone in this room has the same father. Know what that means?"

"You're my brothers and sisters," Dayla said with such a matter-of-fact tone that Rana laughed.

"Right." He faced Rana and Levin. "Can she meet them?"

Levin nodded. "We'll keep looking around and come back for her when we're done or when we find something. Do you want to do that, Dayla?"

Dayla smiled at Mallory. "Yeah. That sounds fun."

"Okay. We'll see you later."

Dayla and Mallory walked to a table where Mallory had sprawled pieces of a jigsaw puzzle. Rana followed Levin into the hall, hoping their search would be short-lived.

Chapter Eighteen

Levin pointed down the hall. "I'm guessing we'll find more empty rooms this way. Have you seen anyone who works here?"

"No. I was wondering about that."

"Should we go to the first floor? I'm a little worried you'll see someone you know there, too." He winked to her. She scowled at him in return.

They reached a stairwell at the end of the hall and headed downstairs. Levin poked his head out the door.

The first floor looked nothing like the other two. The rooms teemed with people–employees–working together at tables and computers. Nothing suggested any kind of scientific testing was occurring.

The windows between the rooms and the hall made it easy to see what the employees did, but they also made it easy for the employees to see uninvited guests snooping around. A woman made eye contact with Levin, pointed at him, and yelled something, but he closed the door and told Rana to run up the stairs before he heard what she said.

With his heart racing, Levin yanked open the door on the third floor and bumped into a large man standing on the other side. He towered over both siblings and looked like he lifted weights for fun.

"You two need to come with me." His voice boomed through the stairwell. Levin swallowed, guessing the guy could pick him up and throw him with little effort.

The man held the door open, and they joined him in the hall. "Go to the elevators."

He walked behind them past the room that housed their siblings. Levin glanced inside and made eye contact with Brent and Scott. The man pushed them onto the elevator, though he didn't physically touch them. He pressed the button labeled "B."

"Where are we going?" Levin asked.

The man stood in silence. Levin tried to swallow the lump in his throat.

The elevator opened into a dimly-lit corridor, and the man pointed to the right. "Walk to the room at the end of the hall."

They left the elevator and walked with the man following close behind. When they reached the door, the man reached between them and unlocked it.

The room was large enough to hold a sizable group and contained no furniture. A short stage stood against the far wall, and the fluorescent lights, gray carpet, and dark gray walls gave the space a cave-like feeling.

"Wait here." The man left the room and locked the door behind him.

Rana and Levin looked at each other. Levin pulled his phone from his pocket. "Damn. No signal." He clenched his jaw.

Rana walked towards the stage. "Now what?"

"Good question." He joined her in examining the space. Rana opened a door on the same wall as the door leading to the hallway. "That's a restroom."

"I wonder how long they're planning to keep us down here." Levin walked to a door next to the stage, opened it, and found an empty closet. He walked to the middle of the room, crossed his arms, and stared at one of the walls. "I guess we wait for someone else to come in the way we did and find out what's going on."

****

Rana sat with Levin against a wall and asked, "Do you think Mom is here?"

Levin rubbed his neck. "Yeah, I do. They're just seeing what they can do with us before we find her."

"Why?"

"Probably to make us think they control us. We've done everything they wanted us to do since they took Mom, so in a way, they have controlled us. After we find her, though..." He shook his head and glared at the opposite wall, "We should all drop off their radar. Go somewhere really remote, you know? I'll get Maggie back, and we'll make a new life."

"Are you going to marry her?" Rana smiled teasingly at him.

"I hope so." He gazed at his shoes, though obviously not thinking about his shoes.

The door opening startled Rana. The large man escorted Brent, Isaiah, and Jeremy inside. Levin jumped to his feet and walked two steps before the man closed the door and locked it.

Jeremy approached them. "Levin, what is this place?"

He glared at the locked door. "I don't know. That door is the only way out."

Brent and Isaiah explored the room, just as Levin and Rana had done when they first arrived.

"What's the stage for?" Isaiah asked from across the room.

"Maybe they'll put on a show for us later." Rana laughed.

Brent left the empty closet and joined the group. "W…w…where's Dayla?"

"We found a group of PR kids on the second floor who have the same father she does. We left her there so she can get to know them. We planned to go back for her." He shook his head. "I hope she isn't scared." He turned his attention to Jeremy. "Did you leave Eliot in the room?"

Jeremy nodded. "Brent and Scott saw the big man leading you two down the hall. Scott left right away saying he wanted to find out what happened. The three of us waited ten minutes before deciding to find you ourselves. I told Eliot to stay behind. The big guy found us on the second floor and brought us here."

"I wonder if that's what they're doing," Levin said. "Waiting for us to leave–to disobey their directions–before intercepting us. We might not know their plan until everyone's here."

"That could take a while," Jeremy said.

The five sat in a circle on the floor. Rana and Isaiah compared high school experiences, and Jeremy shared funny stories about his P.E. students. Brent listened. Levin sat facing slightly away from the group and towards the door without contributing much to the conversation and drumming his fingers on his leg.

Rana took her phone from her pocket and checked it. "We've been here for almost two hours. I'm hungry."

"So am I. When the big guy makes his next delivery, we can ask him to bring us some food." Levin stood and walked closer to the door. The rest of the group followed, and everyone sat back in their circle.

Half an hour later, the door made noise. A different man–this one also large and intimidating–led a group of people with dark brown skin into the room. Levin jumped up before the man closed the door. "Sir, we need some food."

The man studied Levin before shutting the door.

A few minutes later, the man returned carrying large, canvas bags. He put them on the floor and left again, locking the door behind him.

Rana looked into one of the bags. "There's a lot of bread in here–like twenty loaves." She looked into the other bag. "This one has jars of peanut butter and jelly." She dug into the bag and removed three plastic knives.

Levin took one of the knives from her and faced the group. "Who's hungry?"

Levin and Rana prepared sandwiches, and the group members talked while they ate their meager meal. Rana did the math: based on the amount of food they were given, at least fifty more people would show up eventually. That, or this food was supposed to last a while. What could they be planning that required everyone to gather in a large group?

"Do you guys know where your father lives?" Jeremy asked between bites.

A woman who appeared Levin's age answered, "Yeah, he's American. He lives in New England somewhere, but they wouldn't tell us where exactly. Do you guys all have the same father?"

"We do. He's Greek. They didn't tell us exactly where in Greece, either."

She laughed.

"What were you doing when the big guy caught you?" Levin asked.

An older boy answered, "We got tired of waiting in that room. We decided to look around. He found us in the hall."

"Did you leave anyone behind in your room?" Rana asked.

"Yeah. We left the younger ones with my sister. She's sixteen."

"Do any of you know why we're here?" Levin asked.

The older woman answered again after a few silent seconds. "Well, we thought they wanted to do genetic testing. I'm starting to doubt that, though. Seems like they're pulling everyone together for some reason."

The door opened as she finished speaking. The man who brought in Levin and Rana reappeared, this time escorting a group of five tall kids with reddish-brown hair. One of the boys covered his nose with a paper towel.

Jason jogged to Rana. "Oh, there you are. Dayla thought you forgot about her. I told her we would look for you, but Gigantor found us and brought us here."

"What happened to your nose?" Levin asked the injured boy.

"I tried to run past the big guy. He hit me."

Rana swallowed. Apparently, PR wanted them all in this room badly enough to use force. That would make an escape more difficult.

The day slowly passed as the room's population grew. Four hours after Rana and Levin arrived, Dayla appeared with what looked like the remaining members of Jason's group. By then, around forty people occupied the space. They had spent the previous hours in furnished rooms surrounded by empty rooms in different parts of the building.

Rana scanned the crowd, counting on her fingers and categorizing.

Jason approached her. "So bored you decided to do math?"

"I'm figuring out how many fathers we represent." She pointed to the different groups. "Greek, Scottish, American, Chinese, Venezuelan. And I bet more will show up."

"Why do you think they chose fathers from all over the world? Looks like the mothers all live in the U.S."

Rana shrugged. "Maybe the Project Renovatio organizers planned it that way to make the fathers hard to find. Or to make the mothers easier to monitor."

As the hours passed, the group grew increasingly restless. Arguments occurred between some of the siblings, and a few of the younger kids cried. Rana wrung her hands. They wouldn't handle being locked up much longer.

There had to be a way out.

She wandered to the stage and examined its floor and the wall behind it. There were no seams in the carpeting. The closet next to the stage appeared intact; each wall was sturdy and without cracks. Maybe they could climb through the ceiling tiles in the bathroom.

As she headed that direction, the others from the third floor joined them. Janie and Dayla found each other immediately. Daniel scanned the room, connecting with Levin, Brent, and Jeremy when they waved him over. Levin pointed towards the door and leaned towards his brothers.

They're planning something.

In a few minutes, Levin led them to where most of the others had settled on the floor.

"I would like to leave. Is anyone else interested in doing that?" he asked loudly enough to get everyone's attention. He clasped his slightly trembling hands in front of him.

Many nodded, while others said "Yeah" or "Please."

"We have an idea. Enough of us are here now to fight off whichever big guy arrives next and escape."

The woman with the American father raised her hand. "We still have family in our room. How do we get them out?"

"We'll need to move quickly. Here's the plan: when 'Gigantor' opens the door," he paused for the giggling to subside, "Jeremy, Daniel, and I will push him into the hall and hold him. Brent will lead the rest of you past us. Don't look back. Get as many on the elevator as you can." He looked at the woman. "Start with those of you with family in one of the rooms. After you get them, take the stairs to the first floor. I think there's an exterior door you can use by the stairwell."

While everyone stood, the three men waited by the door for their opportunity. Rana claimed a spot at the back of the group, and her nerves gathered in her stomach. This had to work. She picked at her fingernails as the minutes ticked by and watched Levin wipe his hands on his shorts.

The lock clicked, and the door pushed open. Levin didn't wait for them to enter the room. He curled his head and slammed himself shoulders first into Gigantor's chest. His brothers joined him, pushing against the man's arms and shoulders. They knocked him down and pinned him to the floor.

"Go," Levin yelled. The kids ran past the brothers. Brent led the group, and Rana brought up the rear.

Gigantor squirmed and grunted but stopped long enough to say something. "It's no use."

"What do you mean?" Levin pressed his full weight into the guy's shoulders.

"Trying to escape. They need a key to open the elevator. And I'm wearing a wire. The people upstairs can hear everything. Someone will meet them at the elevators."

"We can't open the elevators," Isaiah yelled from the front of the group.

The man chuckled. A moment later, the elevator doors opened, revealing the other big man. He pointed a shotgun at Brent's face.

****

Two hours after the gun-toting man pushed everyone back inside, the room's population had doubled. Rana couldn't believe the big guys allowed Levin and his brothers to return to the group with no reprimand. Apparently, PR didn't view them as a threat.

The last detainees to arrive said they'd planned to leave when the big guys intercepted them. They represented three more areas from around the globe: Canada, Egypt, and Russia. A few mothers sat among the young members of the crowd, and Rana assumed that like Jason, most of the older siblings brought the younger ones by themselves.

The new arrivals helped themselves to the remaining peanut butter and jelly ingredients while they waited to learn what the Project Renovatio people planned to do with them. Twenty minutes after the last group arrived, the door opened again. A middle-aged, bald man wearing Dockers and a burgundy golf shirt entered, walked across the room, and stood on the stage. The kids sitting on the stage joined the others on the floor. The man stood silently, studying them all.

When everyone quieted, he raised his arms. "Welcome. Welcome to all of you." He clasped his hands in front of him. "It has been a long day of waiting, but you're all finally here." The man sounded exhausted or relieved. Rana couldn't decide which.

"My name is Peter. I've been a part of Project Renovatio from the beginning. In fact, my work resulted in many of you being born." He scanned the audience. "We've worked to get you all together for nearly six months. The method, of course, presented a challenge. We didn't want to just . . . *send* invitations. You are special. You are bright. The way in which you arrived had to be unique."

"You tricked us," a young man near the stage yelled.

"Yes, we did. In receiving the letters, those of you who didn't know about the Project would have to learn, and you would all have a strong reason to come here at the same time. We let you wait in the rooms long enough for you to challenge us. We wanted to see how long it would take, so we know how to handle you in the future." He looked towards Rana and Levin. "For some of you, it didn't take very long." He grinned, nodded, then turned his attention to the group.

Rana whispered to Levin, "That's not why we're here. I think he knows it."

"Of course he does."

Peter continued, "It's my pleasure to introduce you to someone else, someone very important to our vision. He will explain the rest." Peter held his arm towards the door, and everyone turned their heads.

Rana gasped when Scott entered the room and approached the stage.

Chapter Nineteen

Levin sat up straighter. "What the hell?" Aside from those who had been in the third floor waiting room, the audience appeared oblivious to the significance of Scott's presence.

Scott joined Peter on the stage. Peter shook Scott's hand and retreated to the floor. Scott wore a wide smile. "Thank you, Peter. I know some of you are surprised to see me here." He looked at the corner where Levin sat with his brothers and their siblings then turned his attention to the middle of the group.

A foul taste sat in the back of Levin's throat, and his stomach turned. He'd mindlessly allowed himself and all of his siblings to be fooled.

"For the rest of you, allow me to introduce myself. My name is Scott. Like you, I am a child of Project Renovatio, and I am the lead in this current project of bringing you all together." He paced on the stage. "You see, we believe if you–we–join forces, combine our intelligence and strength, well…" He glanced at his shoes and chuckled.

"Let me start over. We are on a journey, a journey towards dominance, and it starts today. If we execute our plan the way we expect, our children and grandchildren will want for nothing. The creators of Project Renovatio designed us to build our own society. To rule. And we're finally in the position to fill that purpose." He scanned the crowd and lifted his chin a little. "You represent a fourth of all PR kids. Three other groups like you are meeting in other locations. Soon, we will bring everyone together." He smiled. "Our ability to survive in less than favorable circumstances will make us unstoppable."

Levin clenched his fist and breathed harder the longer Scott spoke. How could Scott's plan combined with this group in this place result in a positive outcome? Surely, no one would join Scott, and in that case, how would they get out of here?

He glanced at the door. One of the large men stood guard in front of it, holding the shotgun.

Scott preached to a captive audience.

"It has been an interesting time, organizing and eagerly awaiting this moment. Some of us suffered injury in the pursuit of our goal." Scott rolled the right sleeve of his shirt, revealing a bandage that circled most of his upper arm, and stared at Levin. "But such a great purpose will certainly not come without sacrifice."

Levin jumped to his feet and rushed towards Scott, his heart pounding in his ears. "What did you do with her? And how could you claim to help us, and then…this!" He stopped near the front of the stage and towered over the still-seated crowd.

Scott smiled. "Your mother tried to remove herself and your family from any involvement with PR. We had to do something. We don't want anyone thinking they can 'quit' PR, not when there's so much work to do."

"Work to do? Have you lost your damned mind? You don't own us, and you can't make us work for you."

Shouts of agreement moved through the crowd.

Scott focused on Levin. "Of course we own you! We're the reason you exist." The group quieted at his volume. He continued in a softer tone. "Do you think anyone outside PR, who can't understand us, will accept us? Please. We can be outcasts," he spread his arms and faced the crowd, "or we can claim our place of superiority. Now," he looked at Levin, "what do you think we should do?"

Levin pointed at Scott and took two steps towards the stage. "First, you should tell me where my mother is. Then, you should let everyone here live the lives they choose."

The crowd cheered him, boosting his confidence. He took a breath and another step. "Tell me!"

"Your mother?" Scott sneered. "You don't need to worry about her anymore."

"You're lying. That's all you've done until now." The crowd quieted again. "My mother cut off PR because *you* told us to do that."

"I tested you. We need to know where your families' loyalties lie. Only your mother tried breaking communication, so," he scanned the crowd, "we made an example of her."

Levin jumped onto the stage and smashed his fist into Scott's jaw. The impact sent a shock wave up his arm. Stumbling backwards, Scott brought his hand to his face, then reached into his pocket and removed a knife, clutching the handle in his fist. He snapped it open and lunged.

Levin blocked with his arm. Scott forced it down, drove the blade into the flesh near Levin's shoulder and dragged it over his skin, ending at his stomach. He pulled it away and stepped back.

Heat rushed to the wound. Levin yelled and hunched over, bringing his hand to his chest. Blood soaked into his sliced shirt and dripped onto the floor. He eyed Scott's taunting glare, then the knife in Scott's hand, and collapsed.

A deafening boom echoed through the space.

****

Rana shut her eyes and covered her ears to protect them from the noise. When she opened her eyes, she thought she was dreaming.

"Mom!" She jumped to her feet. Her mother stood at the back of the stage by the empty closet, pointing a gun towards the place Scott had stood. Her arms shook violently. A man who looked familiar stood behind her. Scott, bleeding from a wound on the back of his head, lay on the stage near Levin. The crowd sat in shocked silence.

Dayla rushed past Rana. Seeming to snap out of a trance, Liz passed the gun to the man standing behind her, stepped off the stage, and opened her arms to receive her younger daughter.

Rana swallowed the lump in her throat and ran to Levin. Daniel and Jeremy were quick to follow. Their brother lay curled on his side in the fetal position, squirming as blood ran from the wound and down his arm. Daniel shoved on Levin's shoulder, and Levin moaned.

"Come on, let us help you," Daniel said.

Levin uncurled, lying on his back.

Daniel widened the cut in the shirt and scrunched his nose. "It's deep. I'll need to find something to stitch him up." Putting his fingers into the sliced fabric, he tore Levin's shirt enough to remove it, then bunched it up and used it to apply pressure to the gaping wound.

As Daniel worked, the man holding the gun took the stage next to Scott's body. He dropped to his knees, putting his fingers on Scott's neck, and shook his head. Inhaling a shaking breath, he rose to standing.

The two large men held Peter's arms. One of them stuck a needle full of something into Peter's neck that made him pass out.

The man on the stage eyed the gun in his hand. "I'm Dr. Steven Craig." He looked at Scott, then Levin, then to the group. "Come with me. I'll explain everything to you soon, but we need to get you out of here right now. There are vans waiting outside to take you to a safe location. Please, follow me."

"Why should we do that? Your people have led us around all day," an older boy yelled. Shouts of agreement moved through the crowd.

Dr. Craig held out his hand, as if trying to calm the group. "I don't have time to explain everything now. Scott was not working with us. He has people upstairs expecting you to join them. They want to initiate you into some kind of army. We need to leave before they realize what's happened, or your lives will be in danger. You have to trust us."

Dr. Craig walked into the storage closet, followed by Rana's mother and Dayla. Rana thought back to when she examined the space. The door had been well hidden.

She looked at Levin and then to Jeremy. "How do we get him out of here?"

Levin squirmed. "I can walk."

Jeremy jumped onto the stage, put his arm around Levin's back, and placed Levin's arm around his own shoulders. He lifted Levin to his feet. Daniel kept the pressure on the wound with the shirt as the men stood. Levin winced and took small steps. By the time they moved, the entire group worked their way towards the closet. Jeremy and Daniel helped Levin walk across the stage.

Rana glanced at the crowd. Jason stood still, watching her.

He met her at the stage, looked at Levin, then back to her. "Will he be okay?"

She nodded. "Daniel said he could stitch him up." She walked with Jason towards the door, behind her brothers.

"How do you think your mother escaped?" he asked.

Rana shrugged as tears welled in her eyes.

Jason stopped walking and put his hand on her shoulder. "Can I give you a hug?"

She laughed through her tears. “Yeah. Sure.” He wrapped his arms around her and pulled her close. She sobbed into his shirt.

He squeezed her. “Come on. We have to go.”

She nodded and released, focusing on the retreating group. “They’re all like us, aren’t they?”

Jason met her eyes. “Yeah. And we need to join them.”

They entered the closet after everyone else. A brick propped open a door that had been the right wall. They walked through a skinny corridor, to a ladder leading through a window well, and climbed into fresh air.

The night sky surprised Rana. “I can’t believe how long they kept us in there.”

“It was a long day.”

Rana scanned the row of passenger vans; her mother stood by the one in front. Jason turned the other direction. “I see my sister in that other van. I’ll catch up with you when we get to wherever we’re going.”

She grabbed his wrist. “Is this safe? How can we trust them?”

“I think so. I mean, that was your mother, right?” He gave her shoulder a squeeze and walked towards his van.

Rana ran towards hers. Her mother opened her arms. Rana crashed into her mother so hard they both laughed. Her mother took Rana’s face in both hands, kissed her on the forehead, and brought her back into the hug.

“I’m glad you’re okay.” Rana’s words sounded woefully inadequate.

“Thanks, honey. I missed you so much.”

"Mom, I need to ask you a question before I get in the van."

Her mother released Rana from the hug. "What's that?"

"Why did you have us?"

Her mom took a second to answer. "What do you mean?"

"Was it for the money? Or because the Project wants us to get married and have kids? Do you work for them? I'm just . . . not sure what to believe."

"Rana, I had you because I wanted to, and because I knew I would love you. Trust me, and trust Dr. Craig. Scott was behind everything that happened. You heard what he said." She hugged Rana again. "I wouldn't let you get in this van if I didn't think it was safe. In fact, I think *not* getting in this van is dangerous." She gestured to the van with a head tilt.

Rana climbed aboard.

The dome lights illuminated the interior. Dayla faced backwards on her knees in the front row.

Levin lay across two seats while Daniel squeezed himself in the small space between that row and the one in front. Rana took the seat behind Levin.

His face was pale and held a pained grimace. He rested his arm across his forehead and closed his eyes.

Rana's mother took an empty seat in front of Levin and Daniel and turned herself to face them. She covered her mouth with her hand and silently cried when she saw her son.

"Daniel got a fff…first aid kit from the d…d…driver," Brent said from the seat next to Rana's.

"Yeah, the box had a suture kit but no lidocaine, so Levin has to bear this out 'til I finish." Daniel winced as he stitched the wound. "You hanging in there, buddy?"

Levin answered with a moan. Several medical pads coated in blood sat on Levin's shorts. His blood-soaked shirt rested under his side.

The driver twisted around. "Are you almost done? I need to turn the lights off so we can leave."

"Not really, but go. I'll manage," Daniel said. "Does anyone have a flashlight?"

The lights went out and the van moved. Rana took her phone from her pocket, turned on her flashlight app, and shined the light on Levin's side. Daniel held his arms over Levin as if assessing how the van moved before continuing on the wound.

"Do you know what you're doing?" Rana asked.

"Yeah, I'm in medical school, remember?" He glanced at her. "Don't worry; I know the basics of suturing." He returned his attention to the wound. "The cut doesn't go deeper than the muscle. His organs are fine. That's the good news."

"What's the bad news?"

"Well, the kit didn't have much to control infection. Just some little alcohol pads and a small bottle of iodine. We can only hope that's good enough at the moment."

"I guess this will test that stronger immunity we're supposed to have," Rana said.

"Yeah. Good point." As Daniel stitched his way across the wound, Levin occasionally winced, groaned, held his breath, and exhaled slowly.

"Levin, look at me," his mother said.

He opened his eyes and focused on her.

"You're going to be fine. Do you hear me?"

He nodded and closed his eyes, sending tears down the sides of his face. She reached over the back of her seat and wiped them with her thumb.

After watching them for a minute, Rana needed a distraction. “Mom, what happened to you? How did you end up with Dr. Craig?”

Her mother wiped the tears from her face with her free hand. “Well, on Saturday night, someone rang the doorbell. When I answered it, two hooded guys pushed their way in. Scott grabbed me and tried to bring me to the floor. I cut him with my ring and ripped his hood off. I must have nicked an artery because he bled like crazy. I thought I could fight him off, but his partner came over and stuck a needle in my neck. Whatever he injected made me pass out. I woke tied up in the back of a utility van. Scott was gone, but the other guy drove–the same guy who introduced Scott tonight.”

“Peter?” Jeremy asked from across the row.

“Yes, him.”

“Scott stayed in Denver so Levin could pick him up at the airport,” Rana figured.

“Makes sense. Anyway, he drove me to the building we just left. Some other people locked me in one of the rooms. They basically left me alone until yesterday, when Dr. Craig found me. He opened the door and gestured for me to follow him. He led me through a few hallways and out a side door, took me to a car, and drove me to a motel.

“On the way, he told me the Project Renovatio staff split a year ago. Scott and his supporters forced Dr. Craig and his supporters out of the organization. The part Scott led was hell-bent on getting all the PR kids together to form an army. Dr. Craig said he needed my help to rescue you." She moved her attention to Levin when he winced. She stroked his hair.

Rana wrapped her arms around the seat in front of her. "Did you know you would have to kill Scott?"

She pursed her lips. "Not exactly. We waited until he and Peter started talking because we couldn't know before then if all the PR kids were there. We peeked out at the same time Levin punched Scott, and we made our move after Levin collapsed." She took a shaking breath. "We didn't know if the gun would be a sufficient threat or if we would need to use it." She wiped her face with her open hand. "Dr. Craig told me to fire when I had a clear shot."

"Why didn't he shoot Scott?" Jeremy asked.

"He didn't think he could shoot his own son. Well, the man he raised as his son. He knew hesitating would put you all at risk."

"How did Dr. Craig know what Scott planned if Scott forced him out of PR?" Rana asked.

"He had some people working for him who appeared to work for Scott–those two big guys who led you to the room, among a few others. They kept Dr. Craig updated about Scott's plans, and they made sure all of you ended up in that room, because that was the exit point."

"Now I feel bad for tackling one of them." Jeremy chuckled.

"Okay, that should do it," Daniel said while examining his handiwork. "It's not pretty, but it should hold." He faced Levin. "Lie around as much as you can until it heals enough for me to remove the stitches. If you pull on them, it will hurt and you could open them. Then we'll have to do this all over again." He covered the wound with gauze and medical tape.

"Thank you," Levin muttered. "Does anyone have an extra shirt?"

****

Levin relaxed after Daniel finished the stitches. Daniel found an empty seat on the opposite side of the van and fell asleep. A pang of guilt hit Levin's stomach when he remembered thinking Daniel was obnoxious when they first met.

He couldn't see anyone else from his position. Silence filled the dark van.

A steady burning sensation remained across his left side, and the van seats itched his back. He planned to ask someone to buy painkillers and a shirt when they stopped for gas. If they stopped for gas. He still had no idea where they were going.

He pulled his phone from his pocket, checked the time, and sent a text to Maggie despite the late hour. He needed to talk to her, but he didn't know where to start.

Mom is back with us. He waited a few minutes and started to think she'd gone to sleep when he received her reply.

That's so great! What happened?

Long story. Lots of PR kids are with us now. We're headed somewhere. He considered telling her about his injury but decided against it. He didn't want to worry her.

Where are they taking you?

I don't know.

How long will you be gone?

I don't know.

Can I go home?

He wiggled his thumbs as he contemplated his answer. He decided to ask someone who knew better than he did. “Mom, are you awake?”

She twisted around and peered over the back of her seat.

“Is it safe for Maggie to go home?”

“Go home? Where is she?”

“I sent her to her uncle’s place in Arizona after you disappeared.”

“Oh. She’ll be fine. I don’t think anyone besides Scott knew about her.”

Levin sighed. *Mom says it’s safe for you to go home.*

A few moments passed before she replied.

Okay. I’ll leave tomorrow. See you soon?

I hope so. I love you.

I love you, too.

He started to pocket his phone when his mother stopped him.

“Can I use that? I want to call Walt and tell him I’m okay.”

“Sure.” He handed her the phone, closed his eyes, and tried to fall asleep in spite of the fiery pain coming from his ribcage.

Chapter Twenty

Rana woke as the van stopped at a gas station. The sun peeked over the horizon. Where were they?

"Good time for a break. Everyone out," the driver said.

The passengers unloaded. Rana looked over the seats in front of her. Levin slept, taking long, deep breaths. She considered letting him rest but didn't know when they might stop again. She shook his shoulder until he stirred.

"What? Are we there?" he asked in a groggy voice.

"No. We stopped at a gas station. The driver suggested everyone take a break."

"Okay." Levin glanced at his torso. "I need a shirt." He pulled his wallet from his pocket and gave Rana a credit card. "If they have shirts, buy one for me. Get some painkillers, too."

"Okay." She took the card and left the van.

The gas station displayed souvenirs that said *Utah* on them. Rana picked a generic blue shirt in what she guessed was Levin's size, ibuprofen, and sodas. She paid, looked towards the restroom, and decided to take the items to Levin to give the line a chance to shrink. Their driver stood next to the van.

"Hi. I'm Rana."

"Hi, Rana. I'm Aaron." He scratched his goatee.

"Where are the other vans?" she asked.

"Every driver took a different route. We'll all end up in the same place, though."

"And where's that?"

"You'll see. We have a full day of driving ahead of us. You might want to go buy yourself a book." He stared at her. "Is your brother the injured guy?"

"Yeah."

He nodded. "He looked pretty bad last night. Did the doctor guy do a good job stitching him up?"

She remembered him asking last night if they needed to stop at a hospital. "I think he did fine. Levin's in pain, but I bought him something for that." She lifted the bag. "I should get it to him."

"Okay. See you in the van in a few minutes."

She climbed through the side door and found her brother sitting up. She gave him his credit card and pulled the shirt from her bag.

He took it from her. "We're in Utah?"

"I guess. Aaron, the driver, said we'll be driving all day but he didn't tell me where we're going. He said the other vans took different routes to the same place."

"Huh." He put the shirt over his head and groaned as he lifted his arm. Rana grabbed the sleeve and helped him ease his arm through it.

"I got you these, too." She handed him the ibuprofen and one of the sodas.

"Thanks." He swallowed some pills.

"Wanna go inside with me? There's food. I think Mom and Dayla need you to pay since Mom doesn't have her wallet. I can bring your card to them if you want to stay here."

"I'll come in." He held the seats in front of him and pulled himself to his feet. The two left the van and walked to the building. Levin kept his arm bent and close to his side.

****

When they arrived at a campground, the sky glowed orange from the sunset. The road signs indicated they'd crossed into Montana hours earlier. Aaron took them to a department store in the last town, where he purchased clothes and toiletries for all of them.

The area reminded Rana of where she used to go to summer camp. Bigger buildings surrounded a central area with a large fire pit, and smaller buildings scattered the outer edges of the property.

"Looks like we're the first ones here." Aaron parked the van by one of the larger buildings. Everyone piled out and wandered the grounds.

"Rana, why are we here?" Dayla asked as the group huddled near the fire pit.

"I don't know, girlie."

"This is an old campsite." Aaron peered into the pit. "Kids used to come here for summer programs.

The owners sold it to Dr. Craig. He realized as Scott's plan unfolded that he may need a large place for you kids to stay for a while."

Eliot asked, "Do you work for Dr. Craig?"

"Yes. I worked on the last phase of the Project. When Scott started recruiting PR staff, Dr. Craig pulled me aside to tell me Scott would force him out. I told him I would stand with him. About half of the original PR staff works with Dr. Craig. He's planning on telling everyone the rest of the story after they arrive. We took the quicker route because of our injured passenger; the rest should get here in the next three hours. Those cabins are unlocked. Go have a look around."

"Sir, how long will we stay here?" Jeremy asked.

"Until it's safe for you to leave."

****

Levin claimed a bottom bunk in one of the cabins and tried to sleep until he had a reason to be up. As long as he stayed unconscious, his wound didn't throb.

"Everyone's h…h…here now." Brent's voice pulled Levin out of his shallow slumber.

"Okay. I'll walk with you." Levin grabbed the bedrail above him and lifted himself while Brent waited by the door.

The men walked along the dirt path to where the group gathered around the fire pit, where tall flames now blazed. When Dr. Craig looked in their direction, he announced, "Everyone, please take a seat." A half circle of bench-like seats faced the fire. Levin and Brent claimed spots in the front row.

Dr. Craig stood in front of the fire; his casual outfit contrasted with the seriousness of the moment. "I wish I could say I'm glad to see you all here, but that's not entirely true. It means we've reached our last option. It means we couldn't stop Scott and his supporters before now. And for that, I apologize." He stared blankly in front of him and cleared his throat.

"A year ago, Scott managed to convince a little more than half of the PR employees that we planned to create an army of genetically superior soldiers. He told a beautiful and untrue story about how that was the plan all along, and I was too slow and incompetent to implement it. He even suggested I worked for a secret agency with the mission of eliminating PR kids because they could overthrow the government."

Mild laughter moved through the group.

"He planned to go around to the PR kids, tell them about their unique genetic situation, and persuade them to join him in his cause. He quickly figured out talking to every PR family individually would take a very long time. So, he came up with the plan to lure you all into a large group."

Dr. Craig paced in front of the pit. "A few months after he started recruiting without my knowledge, he had enough supporters from my staff that he could forcefully remove me and anyone who supported me. I had a few days' warning before he ousted me, though, and I moved some of the Project money into a secret account, which I've set up to receive a portion of any future funding. Our supporting governmental departments keep us well financed, and I've hidden quite a lot of it without anyone noticing. I used the money to buy this property, and we have plenty of food and supplies for you all to live here for a while. Some of my former PR staff will prepare food and wash linens. You'll figure out the rest as you go along."

A girl raised her hand, and Dr. Craig faced her. "Yes, do you have a question?"

"Yes. I'm confused. Scott's dead. Why do we need to stay here?"

He rubbed his neck and cleared his throat before answering. "Great question. He scattered his supporters around the country. Some stayed in San Diego, but the rest he had stationed around PR families. We don't know what they will do now that he isn't around to lead them." He paused and cleared his throat again, as if to keep from crying. "We're keeping you all here until we're sure they don't pose a threat to you."

He directed his attention towards Levin. "You've all seen that Scott didn't shy away from violence. He taught his followers to use violence when necessary to grow their cause. Because of that, another leader could rise up to continue Scott's mission. We want to make sure that doesn't happen."

Another teenager's hand went up. "Do we have to stay here? And for how long?"

"I can't force you to stay, but I can't promise your safety if you leave. Scott's supporters will likely want revenge and will take it out on you. Scott presented himself as a general. His supporters will take his death very hard. To answer your other question, you'll stay as long as it takes for my people to neutralize the threat. We're finding and influencing Scott's people every day. To complicate matters, we need to reach the other PR kids before Scott's people do. Did Scott say the rest were meeting in large groups like this one?"

A few in the crowd murmured confirmation, and Dr. Craig shook his head. "That's not true. You are the only PR kids he managed to get together. I think he planned to hold separate gatherings for the others."

He paused, as if waiting for more questions, then continued. "You've probably noticed there's no cell phone service here. Tomorrow, we will take you in small groups to the nearest town so you can call your families, jobs, or whoever you need to contact. Assure them you will come home, you just don't know when. Do *not* tell them where you are. You'll all need to turn your phones off after that. The longer they're on, the better the chance one of Scott's supporters will track us. That's all I have for tonight. I'll talk with some of you individually in the coming days. In fact, I'd like Jeremy Ruiz, Levin Davis, Brent Sutherland, and Daniel Jackson to stay behind. Everyone else can get settled in the cabins. Breakfast will be served at 8:30."

The group dispersed, leaving the four brothers clustered around the front row with Dr. Craig sitting among them. Dr. Craig leaned forward with his elbows on his knees. "I thought you guys might have more questions."

"You raised Scott as your son?" Jeremy asked. Levin wondered why, since Jeremy already knew the answer. He decided Jeremy wanted to get Dr. Craig talking.

"Yes, I did. My wife participated in the first phase of the Project. Scott's father was the Greek man, and he was your half-brother. My wife passed away eighteen months ago, and I believe her death sent Scott on this crazy mission of his."

"I'm s…s…sorry for your loss," Brent said.

"Thank you. It's been hard to grieve the loss of my wife with Scott acting the way he was. I hoped it wouldn't come to the conclusion it did last night." He focused on the ground.

"I have a question," Levin said. "Why did Scott do the whole meeting with us? Why didn't he let us learn about PR like everyone else did, with the letter?"

"Did he tell you about the loss of boys in the first phase of PR?"

Levin nodded.

"He saw himself as an elite case because of that. I can't say for sure, but I imagine he wanted to establish a rapport with you before he tried to recruit you to his cause. Perhaps he wanted to make you guys the upper ranks of his force, so to speak."

"And how did kidnapping my mother help him with that?"

"He made it look like I was responsible and he was there to help you, so he would earn your trust. His plan probably changed after I found your mom. He lost his leverage. In the end, it appears he used–or tried to use–her and you to demonstrate what would happen to the others if they went against him."

"Thank you for finding her." Levin's response felt inadequate.

"Sir, I have another question," Jeremy said. "Scott said PR wanted us to marry other PR girls, and our girlfriends would be in danger if we stayed with them. He said you made him break up with his girlfriend. Is that true?"

"No, that's not true. He never had a serious girlfriend, as far as I know. He likely told you that to turn you against me and my supporters, though he called his group PR. My group doesn't have a name. I guess we need to come up with one." He smiled. "But I digress. We designed PR to allow PR kids to grow up and marry whom they choose, because people tend to choose others like themselves as partners. We wanted to create a strong base of people who are able to survive and study how the next generations express their parents' genetic advantages. We obviously didn't get to the second part. We hope to take back the organization at some point and re-establish our research."

A flood of relief covered Levin, and he wished he could call Maggie.

"Well, I'll let you boys get some rest. I'll see you in the morning." Dr. Craig stood and walked towards one of the cabins, leaving the brothers to process the new information.

Jeremy put his arm around Levin's shoulders and offered a huge grin. Levin couldn't help but smile back.

Epilogue

September 7

Today marks the beginning of our sixth week at the camp, and I decided to document our time here. A journal seems the best way to do that. If we end up surviving a global disaster and rebuilding society, this could be in a history book.

Rana stopped writing and laughed at the idea.

Levin's been a giant grump, which I guess I understand. He misses Maggie like crazy, and there's nothing computer related here for him to do, so I think he feels a little useless. Our brothers fill the days with their own skills: Brent fixes anything mechanical, Daniel's become our camp doctor, and Jeremy's formed exercise groups. Levin practices Taekwondo in one of the groups, and he's happier afterwards, but I hope we can go home soon so he'll go back to normal. One of Dr. Craig's guys arrived in Levin's car a week after we did, and I've wondered if Levin will decide to take off one day. I'm a little surprised he hasn't.

Dayla worried she'd fall behind in school, so I asked one of the workers to buy some books for her to study, and I've tried to remember what I learned in fifth grade to help her. The other kids her age caught on to what we were doing, and now I'm running a little school for them. I can't believe how smart they are. I love every second I'm with them, and whenever we do get out of here, I plan to earn my teaching certificate.

She smiled when she imagined the possibility.

We might leave soon, though. Last night, Dr. Craig told us a man named Uriah has taken charge of the people Scott led, and they're back to trying to form an army with the PRs. Dr. Craig wants those of us who are sixteen or older to face Uriah's group. We'll train for ten days, in case we need to fight. I'm not sure ten days are enough for us to do anything, but Dr. Craig said the size of our group will make Uriah's followers see us as an opposing force.

Levin pointed out that Dr. Craig wants to turn us into an army to fight the guys who want to turn us into an army. Dr. Craig told him this is our best chance to go home. Even if we do go home, I wonder if our lives will ever be like they were before we learned about Project Renovatio.

I guess there's only one way to find out.

Continued in Project Liberatio

Did you enjoy the story? Head to the book's Amazon page and write a review! Readers like you make a big difference to writers like me. Thanks in advance!

Acknowledgements

This book would not have been possible without the support of some important people.

First, thanks to my friend and fellow author Carol Bellhouse, whose immeasurable patience, guidance, and encouragement saw me through those rough early drafts. Carol, you will never understand how vital you've been in my growth as a writer.

Second, special thanks to my biggest cheerleaders: my mom and fellow author, Virginia Finnie, and my dear friend Rebecca Mast. If you didn't love everything I write, it would be hard to continue some days. All writers need people like you in their lives.

Also, to my friend and fellow author Dan Alatorre, I can't thank you enough for helping me put the final polish on the story. It's better because of your expertise.

And finally, to my husband, Joe, and our sons, Nathan and Silas, thanks for letting me park at my laptop for countless hours while you played, watched movies, and generally fended for yourselves. Your belief in me and in this new path means everything.

Other Books by Allison Maruska

Drake and the Fliers

"Brilliantly written, you are a part of it all, right from the start. The author's powers of description put you right in the heart of the action with Drake and his friends."

- Amazon Reviewer

Sixteen-year-old Drake can't understand why the virus

spared him. The only survivors he's seen vandalized his makeshift dwelling, and despite his sister's dying wish that he connect with others, he spends his days alone – that is, until he shapeshifts into a dragon.

While exploring his new abilities, Drake nearly flies into Preston, another shifter. Their chances of survival increase if they team up with others like them, but when their search leads to a group in Las Vegas, they find not everyone is welcoming.

As Drake develops new relationships, Preston endures daily confrontation and eventually takes off on his own. Concerned for his friend's safety, Drake launches a search and stumbles into a situation stranger than anything he could imagine. Now he must embrace his animalism if he wants to save his humanity.

"Maruska does a stellar job of creating believable characters that are flawed and relatable but also admirable in their determination." – Allison Gammons, author and blogger for Eclectic Alli

The Fourth Descendant

"Allison Maruska has taken me on an amazing historical adventure in The Fourth Descendant."
-Michelle Stanley, reviewer for Readers' Favorite

When Michelle receives a call from a Richmond historian, she sees the chance for a much-needed adventure. All she has to do is find a century-old key.

Three others – a guitarist, an engineer, and a retiree – receive similar calls. Each family possesses a key to a four-lock safe found buried in a Virginia courthouse, though their connection is as mysterious as the safe itself. Their ancestors should not have interacted, had no apparent reason to bury the safe, and should not have disappeared thereafter.

Bearing their keys, Michelle and the other descendants converge in the courthouse basement and open the safe, revealing the truth about their ancestors - a truth stranger, more deadly, and potentially more world-changing than any of them could have imagined. Now it's up to them to keep their discovery out of the wrong hands.

"I rarely read a story that I can't wait to get back to, and this was one. It's full of drama and suspense. It's fresh and new, something very much needed, and it's totally unpredictable."
- John Darryl Winston, author of IA: Initiate

About the Author

Allison Maruska started her writing adventure in 2012 as a humor blogger. Her first published book, an adult historical mystery novel called The Fourth Descendant, was released in February, 2015. Drake and the Fliers followed in November, 2015. While preparing the Project Renovatio series for publication, she continues to blog, write short stories, and write the standalone sequel to The Fourth Descendant.

Allison recently transitioned to a full-time writing career after working for thirteen years in elementary education. She's also a wife, mom, coffee and wine consumer, and owl enthusiast.

Connect with Allison on the interwebs!

Blog: allisonmaruska.com
Facebook: facebook.com/allisonmaruskaauthor
Twitter: twitter.com/allisonmaruska
Amazon Author Page: amazon.com/author/allisonmaruska

Made in the USA
Columbia, SC
22 November 2021